A crash sounded from the back of the store and Ellie jumped, splashing the contents of the punch bowl up and over the edge.

Her mind flashed to last night. The man slamming her body against the utility sink. His callused hand against her lips. She gasped, a cold fear washing over her.

Johnny moved toward her, a concerned look on his face. He held out his hand, indicating she stay put. Ellie swallowed hard as she watched him disappear into the storage room, her pulse beating wildly in her ears. A few minutes later, he returned with a piece of paper.

Her stomach dropped.

"This was stuffed in the hole of a brick." He tipped his head toward the back door. "There's a nice dent in the middle of the exterior door where he threw it."

Ellie let out a long breath as tiny stars danced in her line of vision. "What does it say?" The words rasped out of her dry throat.

She read over his shoulder. In black angry letters, the wrinkled note read, "Stop playing games or you die."

Alison Stone lives with her husband of more than twenty years and their four children in western New York. Besides writing, Alison keeps busy volunteering at her children's schools, driving her girls to dance and watching her boys race motocross. Alison loves to hear from her readers at Alison@alisonstone.com. For more information please visit her website, alisonstone.com. She's also chatty on Twitter, @Alison_Stone. Find her on Facebook at facebook.com/AlisonStoneAuthor.

Books by Alison Stone

Love Inspired Suspense

Plain Pursuit
Critical Diagnosis
Silver Lake Secrets
Plain Peril
High-Risk Homecoming

HIGH-RISK
HOMECOMING

ALISON STONE

HARLEQUIN® LOVE INSPIRED® SUSPENSE

Recycling programs
for this product may
not exist in your area.

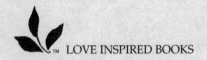 ™ LOVE INSPIRED BOOKS

ISBN-13: 978-0-373-67692-7

High-Risk Homecoming

Copyright © 2015 by Alison Stone

www.Harlequin.com

Printed in U.S.A.

I can do all things through Christ who strengthens me.
–*Philippians* 4:13

For my youngest daughter, Leah Grace, who loves a good storyline as much as her mother. I am proud of you and the person you're becoming. Love you always.

To my husband, Scott, and my oldest three kids, Scotty, Alex and Kelsey. Thank you for being exactly who you are. Love you, always and forever.

ONE

Ellie dropped the paint roller and it landed with a *plop-clack* as the roller landed in the paint and the handle hit the edge of the plastic paint tray. Stepping back, she planted her fists on her hips, and then quickly checked her hands, relieved the bright splotches of paint on her fingers were dry. She resumed her stance and tipped her head, wondering if she should have gone more with the shade Pumpkin Spice and not Citrus Blast. But in the end, all the paint samples had begun to blend together during the height of the gift shop's remodel and, in a fit of decisiveness, she'd chosen Citrus Blast.

"Hmm, when I said our store needed a pop of color, I didn't mean—" her friend and business partner, Ashley, winced and shook her head "—oh…I should have gone with you to the hardware store."

Ellie spun around, biting back her annoyance. Ashley *was* supposed to have gone with her and yet again, she had had a conflict. Ellie took in her friend's cute fall sweater and jeans, and realized Ashley hadn't stopped by to help. She'd probably fib and claim she had a scheduling conflict when in reality, she had a date.

Ashley couldn't hold back a smile. "I have a date, okay?" Ah, she actually admitted it. "I can't help it if you're all work and no play."

Ellie held up her palms to the unpacked boxes and unassembled shelving unit leaning against the adjacent wall. "Our shop *is* having its grand opening tomorrow." She rolled her shoulders, hating the edge to her voice. She was hungry and every muscle in her body hurt. And more than anything, she was tired. So, so, *so* tired.

Ashley shrugged and glanced around. "Everything looks great. Besides, we can't put the shelves up on the back wall until you finish painting." Her friend since the first day of kindergarten dragged a finger along a strand of her smooth blond hair and flipped it over her shoulder. "I told you that wall could wait, but you wanted to have everything perfect for tomorrow."

Ellie angled her head. "Don't you?"

"The shop looks great. We can shove those boxes in the back. No one will see them. Can't those teenage boys from the church help again? They're always looking for volunteer hours." Ashley tapped the cardboard box with the toe of her new boots and rubbed her palms together. "No sense us breaking our backs." Ashley laughed.

Ellie straightened, stretching the crick in her back. What did Ashley know about backbreaking work?

"Oh, you're too much of a perfectionist," Ashley continued. "You'll always find things that need improvement." Her pretty face brightened into a smile. "You need to relax. Have fun. Go on a date."

Ellie forced a laugh. *Go on a date?* Not likely. She wished she could be as easygoing as her longtime friend, but someone had to be the serious one, the planner. Ashley had led a charmed life where everything had been handed to her. Ellie'd had to work for absolutely everything she had and she was done letting others make decisions for her. She was finally taking the reins. Opening her gift shop as she'd always dreamed.

When the right time came, Ellie had reached out to Ashley. Ellie had the vision. Ashley had the financial resources via a trust fund. Their arrangement worked. Ellie liked control and Ashley didn't mind being more or less a silent partner, especially when she had a date or more pressing matters.

Ashley grabbed Ellie's hand and swung it playfully, nearly tugging her arm out of its socket. "Everything will be fine. I promise."

"I do tend to stress." Ellie reclaimed her hand and rubbed her shoulder.

"You're a control freak." Ashley shot her a you-know-I'm-right smile; a smile that always got Ashley exactly what she wanted. "I'm cool with that because I can be spacey sometimes."

Ellie jerked her thumb to the wall separating their shop from the bakery next door. The smells of fresh-baked bread and sweet cupcakes permeated the shop when the paint fumes didn't take over. "Are you going out with Tony again?" Nervous bubbles popped in Ellie's stomach. Tony Vino and his father owned the bakery next door. "Do you think that's a good idea? If things don't work out, you'll have to see him all the time."

Ashley smiled. "You worry too much. Just have fun, can't you? Besides, I promised him I'd treat him to dinner for all the help he's been giving us. Can you imagine if we had to unload all those trucks ourselves?"

How quickly Ashley forgot about all the hard work of the young men from her church. And her brother. Greg had helped unload a truck or two. But now, suddenly, Tony, who seemed to do more flirting than actual work, was the hero in Ashley's eyes.

Ellie rolled her eyes, feigning annoyance. "I have to clean up here. Can you at least come in early tomorrow to help me put up the shelves and unpack the last few boxes?"

"Of course." Ashley tugged on the bottom of her sweater. "Our grand opening is going to be awesome. I have this really cute dress I'm going to wear."

Ashley's enthusiasm vibrated through Ellie. It was this passion that moved Ellie to action. Otherwise she might have still been holed up in her childhood bedroom, stewing over a dead-end job and mourning the breakup with her boyfriend. She blinked slowly, knowing she had dodged a bullet on that one. One of these days, she'd have to track down the poor girl who'd sent her boyfriend romantic texts and send her a thank-you note. If Ellie hadn't casually picked up her boyfriend's dinging cell phone and seen the texts, she might never have known he'd been cheating on her. That had been the pivotal moment. The push she had needed to break up with him, move back to Williamstown and change the direction of her life.

"Okay?" Ashley's impatient tone suggested she had been trying to get Ellie's attention while she was composing a thank-you note she'd never really write.

"I'll be here at 7:00 a.m.," Ellie quickly said to cover up the fact she had been zoning.

"Nine."

"Fine." Ellie's tone was part amusement, part frustration. Why did she bother?

Ashley wiggled her fingers and ran out the front door and Ellie followed her to the exit. A set of bells clacked on the glass, an unnecessary setup considering the alarm system emitted a soft chime every time either the front or back door leading to the alley was opened. Ellie snapped the dead bolt into place and stared out onto quiet Main Street. The crimson-colored leaves on the trees fluttered in the wind and a few drifted to the ground. She loved this time of year.

Crisp nights. Crunchy leaves. Colorful knit sweaters.

She turned around and stepped into the center of her new gift shop. Excitement coursed through her. Finally, tomorrow was the grand opening. She closed her eyes briefly and tried to memorize the moment. Savoring this feeling for if, or more likely *when*, the going got tough.

Then something…a stillness maybe, sent a chill skittering down her spine.

Ellie rubbed her arms. She was tired. Really tired. But a good tired. Her muscles ached from all the physical labor she had done over the past three weeks getting this place ready. All she needed to do was clean up the roller and paint tray and call it a night.

Thwack.

The sharp noise sounded from the storage area. The fine hairs on the back of her neck prickled to life. Holding her breath, Ellie crept toward the storage-slash-office at the back of the store. She was such a chicken.

It's nothing.

Her pulse whooshed in her ears totally not buying the "it's nothing" theory. It didn't help that the exterior door leading to the alley was propped open. Nothing strange there. *She* had propped it open. She hadn't wanted the paint fumes to asphyxiate her. As it was, she had a dull headache thumping at the back of her eyes.

Her attention shifted to the floor. One of the paintings from a local artist that had been resting against the wall was now facedown on the gray concrete floor.

The wind knocked it over, that's all.

Letting out a relieved sigh she sent up a silent prayer of thanks. She picked up the painting and set it on top of a stack of boxes. Boxes she hadn't yet had a chance to sort through. She had given Ashley carte blanche to order for the store, but part of her wondered if they should have agreed on items. If they weren't careful, they'd have more inventory than they could sell. Besides everyday gift-shop wares, they had taken in local work from artists and some unique items from around the world. She'd even included a few older pieces of her own. She longed for the time to create again. Ellie's fingers itched at the thought.

Ellie glanced around the shop one last time. After a few last-minute finishing touches tomorrow, she'd host a reception. A grand opening. She was ready. She had to be. For the first time in her life, she was doing something she wanted to do that wasn't defined by her family. Or a boyfriend.

This was her dream.

She picked up the roller and paint tray, carried them into the storage room and placed them in the utility sink. She removed the broom propping open the back door and the door slammed with a satisfying thud. She turned the bolt and checked the handle again.

Back at the sink, she turned on the hot water and let it run. The water flowed over the paint tray and roller and down into the drain in an orange spiral.

Ellie was eager to go home and get a good night's sleep.

She sensed it a millisecond before she felt it.

Something hard slammed into her. Her knees buckled. A tiny yelp escaped as icy dread swirled in her gut. A prayer floated to mind as automatically as her next breath filled her lungs.

Dear Lord, help me.

A hand clamped over her mouth, jamming her lips against her teeth. A firm arm steadied her, pressing her back against his torso. Heat radiated off his body. Panic and adrenaline surged through her veins. Pushing off the cement floor, she pressed against her attacker, but his rock-hard body forced the solid edge of the utility sink into her belly, making it impossible to move.

Every inch of her scalp prickled with a kind of fear she had never known. The fear humans must experience right before something very, *very* bad was about to happen.

"Don't," she mumbled against his hand.

He pulled her tighter to him. Something sharp on his jacket dug into her back.

"Please don't…" she repeated, unable to see his face.

His warm, uneven breath rasped across her cheek. "Where's the package?" he grunted before a sense of urgency exploded in her. She wrapped her fingers around the handle of the paint roller and brought it up hard and fast. She slugged him in the head with the wet end of the roller.

He backed off with an *oomph* and folded over, his black hood concealing his features.

Ellie bolted toward the entrance to the shop. She tripped over his foot, but regained her balance by grabbing the doorjamb. She swung into the shop.

Muttered curses sounded behind her. Terror charged every possible nerve ending. She ran forward, knees weak, as if she was caught in one of those nightmares where the ground swallowed each foot.

Steps sounded fast behind her.

This was no nightmare. This was real.

Ellie lurched forward and slapped her hand against the panic button on the alarm control next to the front door, a feature her brother had insisted she install. A feature she had thought silly in sleepy little Williamstown, New York, where the biggest crime involved kids and graffiti and a hundred-year-old mill and angry parents who footed the bill for cleanup so junior wouldn't have a police record.

An ear-piercing, strident alarm sounded in the small space. She yanked open the front door. The redundant bells whacked the glass. She tripped over the lip in the doorway. She held out her hands to protect her face from the advancing concrete when two strong hands grabbed her forearms, steadying her.

A scream ripped from her throat.

On the sidewalk in front of Gifts and More, Special Agent Johnny Rock grabbed Ellie Winters and steadied her. Holding her thin, trembling arms, he tilted his head to look into her eyes, but she was squirming, looking frantically behind her.

An ear-piercing alarm split his eardrums.

"Easy there. What's going on? You okay?" He tore his eyes away from her delicate features and scanned the empty shop behind her, his senses heightened.

Her eyes darted around wildly. "Yes, yes, I'm fine." She yanked away from him, fear rolling off her in tense waves.

"I'm not going to hurt you," he reassured her. "What happened?"

Her eyes landed on his and narrowed, something flickering in their depths. She seemed to shake herself. "Someone was hiding in my back room. He attacked me." She lifted her hand absentmindedly to the back of her head. "He...he was chasing me and I..."

"Tripped?" Johnny raised his eyebrows.

"Yes, I tripped over the door frame." Her forehead furrowed as if the blaring alarm was scraping across her nerves. Orange paint splotched the right shoulder of her T-shirt and more was spattered on her face. She pointed toward the back of the shop. "Someone's in there."

"Stay here. I'll check things out." He gently took her forearms and placed her against the brick front between the gift shop's door and the entrance to the bakery. "Don't move."

She reached out, her fingers brushing feather-light against the back of his hand. "No, I don't think you should. Wait for the police." She winced against the harsh sound. "The alarm is tied directly into the police station. They'll be here soon. I hit the panic button."

"I'll be fine." In the chaos, she probably didn't recognize him and realize he was in law enforcement. Last time he had stepped foot in her childhood home more than ten years ago, he had been a friend of her brother's. A friendship that had been doomed from the start because it had been built on false pretenses. Johnny hadn't *really* been a seventeen-year-old transfer student. Johnny had been a twenty-two-year-old rookie cop undercover as a narcotics officer about to rock the tranquil town of Williamstown.

A slam sounded from deep in the shop.

"Stay here," Johnny repeated. "I can't let him get away." *If he hasn't already.* This might be the break in the case he'd been patiently waiting for.

"I really don't think—"

Johnny held up his hand. "Stay here." She flinched at his command. He hadn't meant to snap at her.

He stepped into the shop. Ellie had done a lot of unpacking since the last time he had casually strolled by to check on his target.

With a muscle ticking in his jaw, Johnny pulled his gun from its holster under his jacket. From the doorway to the storage room, he had a clear view of the back exit. Cautiously, he stepped into the storage room. He strained to listen above the blaring alarm. He checked behind the desk, around some boxes and in a small closet. All clear. A paint roller and orange paint sat in a puddle on the floor as if someone had thrown the roller across the room.

Whoever had been here was long gone. He twisted the handle on the back door and found it unlocked. He peered into the alleyway. Other than a large Dumpster and some trash cans, it was empty. He strode over and checked the Dumpster. The pungent smell of garbage clogged his nose, but there was no sign of any stowaway.

The shop's alarm went silent. He returned to the back entrance of the storage room to find Ellie standing in the doorway leading to the shop. She was using the top of her shirtsleeve to wipe at the paint dots on her face. "I turned off the alarm. Police should be here soon." She tucked a strand of hair behind her ear. "He's gone?"

"Yeah."

"Well, thanks for coming to the rescue. The police should be here. You can go." She crossed her arms and studied the gun in his hand. A mix of caution and concern pinched the corners of her mouth.

"I'd rather wait for the police to arrive if it's all right with you."

Ellie rubbed her forearms and narrowed her gaze at him, and seemed to look at him for the first time. *Really* look at him. A shadow of emotion crossed behind her eyes. An emotion he couldn't quite read.

Johnny scratched his forehead and decided he better identify himself. "I met you a long time ago. I was a friend of your brother's." *Was* being the operative word.

"Johnny...Johnny Rock. Yeah, I recognized you as soon as my nerves calmed down and I realized my life wasn't in imminent danger." Her eyes grew dark. "What are you doing here? I thought you moved to Buffalo." The brutal sting of accusation was evident in her tone, suggesting she wished he had stayed in Buffalo.

Johnny tucked his gun back in its holster. "I'm an FBI agent assigned to the Buffalo office."

Ellie made a soft sound at the back of her throat but didn't say anything.

"I'm back in Williamstown to help my grandfather move." It was the truth, but not the entire truth.

Her perfectly groomed eyebrows shot up. "He's selling the house on Treehaven Road?" A faraway look descended into her blue eyes and a smile curved her pink lips. "I always liked that house. I tried to paint it a time or two."

"Paint it?" Johnny's gaze dropped to the up-turned paint tray on the floor.

She laughed.

He liked the sound of it.

Ellie shook her head. "I paint walls out of necessity. I prefer to paint landscapes. On canvas. It's my true calling."

Johnny nodded. "What happened here tonight?"

"I had the door propped open." She shrugged. "Yeah, I know. Stupid." She took in a deep breath, then wrinkled her nose. "I can't stand the fumes. I get migraines. Never thought someone would sneak in and attack me."

He thought he noticed her shiver.

"Are you hurt?" He took a step forward and stopped when she flinched.

"I'm fine."

"Have you had any problems at your shop before?"

She shook her head, her auburn hair with red highlights dropping over one eye. She wrapped her arms around her middle. "I haven't even opened the shop yet." A look—an apology, maybe—crossed her delicate features. A faint splash of freckles dotted her porcelain skin.

"The person who attacked me said something about a package." The color drained from her face.

"Do you know what he was talking about?" Johnny studied her closely.

"No, I have no idea."

"If someone was in here, they exited through the back." He hated to be Captain Obvious, but he didn't know what else to tell her. He pulled open the door and checked the alley again. He had a clear view east to Eagle Street and west to Spring Street. "Whoever was here is long gone." He closed the door and locked it.

Johnny opened his mouth to say something when he noticed a green-and-white police cruiser pull up alongside the curb out front. "The police are here."

Ellie and Johnny walked through the shop and out onto Main Street. The window on the police cruiser slid down. Johnny recognized Officer Mickey Bailey, now a decade older and a few pounds heavier than when they'd first met, but easily identified as the right fielder on the only Williamstown High School baseball team that might have made it to the state championship.

Until the scandal.

Mickey didn't bother to get out of the cruiser, preoccupied as he was with the laptop open on his console. "Alarm go off here?"

"Yes. I shut it off before you arrived," Ellie said, her voice more confident now than when she'd first run out of the shop.

"Hey, Mickey." Johnny approached the cruiser.

Mickey's eye twitched and he looked up from the computer screen. Recognition swept over his ruddy features. His lips tightened as if to say, "Why doesn't it surprise me that you're here?" Mickey collected himself and hid his apparent disdain behind a smug smile. There was no love lost between the two men.

Mickey tapped the door with his open palm, then pushed it open. "Hey there, Johnny. What brings you to town?" The officer stepped onto the sidewalk and pulled on the waistband of his pants.

Johnny wondered briefly if the officer was taunting him. Mickey knew exactly why Johnny was in town. He was here to track the source of illegal drugs. The police department had agreed to keep his presence quiet.

Easier to catch the bad guys that way.

Ellie spoke up before Johnny had a chance. "He's helping his grandfather move."

Johnny detected a bite to her tone.

Mickey jutted his lower lip out and gave her a curt nod. "Is that so?" No doubt, several of the officers resented the FBI working what they considered *their* case. Rumor had it that a few of the officers had had their backsides handed to them in a sling for not tracking down the source of drugs before the nasty stuff claimed the life of a promising high school student.

Johnny jerked his thumb toward the shop. "Ellie was attacked in the back of the shop."

The officer's eyes showed the first sign of interest. "Did you see the guy? Can you give me a description?"

Ellie's cheeks grew flushed and she shook her head, as if she somehow was to blame. "He was wearing a black hoodie, which now has orange paint on it. He was muttering something about a package." She plucked at her own orange-stained T-shirt. "I whacked him with my paint roller."

"Good for you." The officer gave her a once-over that made Johnny suddenly feel possessive; a feeling he didn't have a right to. "You hurt? Need an ambulance?"

Johnny lifted his hand to touch Ellie's back, then thought better of it. His mind flashed to the skinny little girl who used to hang around in the kitchen when her older brother had his friends over. She wasn't the same skinny little girl anymore.

"I'm fine. Just shaken up." Ellie crossed her arms over her midsection and shivered.

"I checked out the shop and the storage area. Whoever was there is gone." Johnny watched Ellie's face turn pink.

The officer strolled toward the door. "I'll check things out." He unfastened the cell phone from his utility belt. "Let me call it in. Maybe someone's seen something." He disappeared into the shop at a slow saunter. The words *big fish, small pond* floated to Johnny's mind.

Ellie turned to follow the officer into the shop. "I need to close up." She went inside and turned the key in the drawer of the register.

"No sign of anyone." Mickey emerged from the back room and tapped his palm on the counter. "You got a mess on the floor with that paint." Leaning heavily on the counter, he lifted a foot, then the other to check the soles of his shoes. "I'll write this up and we'll keep a lookout for this guy. Anything stolen?"

"Not that I can tell," Ellie said as she bent over and slid her purse and sweater out from under the counter.

Mickey pointed at her. "You good?"

"Yeah."

"I'll see she gets home," Johnny said.

"I walked. I'll be fine. I'll clean up the mess in the morning." She glanced around uneasily. "I don't live far."

Johnny took a step closer, refusing to take no for an answer. "Then it won't take me long to walk you home."

A soft breeze blew in over the lake as Johnny and Ellie headed for Eagle Street. Ellie unthreaded her gray sweater from around her purse strap and slipped one arm into it, hoping the paint on her T-shirt had dried. She reached for the other sleeve and Johnny helped her, his knuckles brushing the back of her neck, flooding her with memories. She had had *such* a crush on Johnny Rock. Who wouldn't? He had been the new kid in town. A senior. The all-American high school student. An athlete. She had been the not-so-popular artsy middle school kid.

When they turned onto her street, she slowed. "I can make it the rest of the way from here."

"I'd feel better if I escorted you all the way home."

Inside, her fourteen-year-old self was squealing with delight. *Johnny Rock is walking me home!* Johnny and her brother, four years her senior, had been friends. The best of friends until it was revealed that Johnny was a narc. Her stomach knotted at the harsh reality of that painful time in her family's lives.

"My mom won't be pleased to see you." Anxiety nipped at her fingertips as she sensed the futility of trying to shake him.

"Even after all these years." Johnny's even tone was hard to read.

"Even after all these years," she repeated. Unlike Johnny, Ellie couldn't hide the emotion from her voice. "You ruined my brother's life. You accused him of selling drugs." Her heart pounded in her ears. "You think ten years is long enough to forget that?"

The sound of Johnny's even steps on the gravel made her frustration grow. She was ready to spill over like a Coca-Cola can after it had been shaken.

"Greg didn't go to prison," Johnny finally said, his voice ice and steel.

Ellie grabbed his arm to get his full attention. Johnny stopped walking and looked at her coolly. "My parents spent every last dime on the very best lawyer to prove his innocence."

"Not guilty." Johnny had the nerve to correct her. "There's a difference."

"What are you saying?" She took a deep breath, focusing on controlling her anger, fearing that if she didn't, her loud voice would attract unwanted attention from the neighbors. Her family had been the source of gossip once and she didn't want to go there again. "Still a sore loser after all these years?" Only Roger Petersen, the other teen arrested, had served any jail time. From what Ellie had heard, Roger had maintained his innocence for the duration of his five-year sentence and the five years since his release.

Johnny seemed to catch himself. "The only losers are the kids who get caught up with drugs who then become adults tied up with drugs.

There are no winners there. I'm not happy about any of this."

The reality of what Johnny said diffused some of Ellie's anger. "I know. Drugs are a horrible thing. There was a senior who overdosed a few weeks ago. It's tragic." She ran her hand down her ponytail as her eyes tracked a car traveling down the lonely street. "Maybe they should put another narcotics officer in the high school."

"I'm a little too old to go undercover in the high school again." A corner of Johnny's mouth curved into a grin.

"Of course. I'm not suggesting *you* go undercover." The memory of seeing Johnny—the boy who had befriended her brother, the boy she'd had a crush on, the boy she'd thought was a high school senior—standing on the town hall steps dressed smartly in a police uniform announcing the arrests of the key players on the Williamstown High School baseball team still sent icy dread pulsing through her veins.

Her brother's life had been ruined that day by Johnny's careless accusations. Ellie had never allowed herself to ponder the fact that Roger had actually gone to jail. Had her brother gotten off because of a high-profile lawyer—one whose price had come at the cost of both her and her brother's college educations? She quickly shook away the thought. No, Greg had been innocent.

She didn't know one way or another about Roger. But her brother had been.

"So, you're an FBI agent now?"

Johnny nodded. "Seemed like a good career move."

"Hmm…" Ellie couldn't help but wonder if his career advancement from a small-town cop to an FBI agent came at the expense of others.

"Do you have a problem with that?" Ellie detected amusement in Johnny's tone.

"No," she said, quickening her pace, unwilling to let him crawl under her skin. She had spent a lot of emotion over the years blaming Johnny for the sudden turn her life had taken after her brother's arrest.

A few houses away from her own, Ellie stopped and squared off with Johnny. She gestured with her thumb down the road. "You don't think that… that incident back at my shop was random?"

Johnny gently touched her elbow and coaxed her forward. "He mentioned a package when he attacked you?"

"Yeah. Do you know what that means?" Her heart beat wildly as the soles of their shoes crunched the gravel on the edge of the road. A distant sound of footsteps echoed in her ears. Was someone following them?

Ellie glanced over her shoulder. A long row of

arborvitaes straddling two properties rustled in the wind. A chill crawled down her spine.

Johnny hesitated as if he didn't know what he wanted to say. "The FBI has been tracking a shipment of drugs to your gift shop."

Ellie pressed a hand to her throat. Cold fear washed over her. "My gift shop? I don't understand."

"The FBI was tracking a shipment of drugs to your Main Street address when it went missing." He rubbed a hand over his face and signaled with his head, indicating that they should pick up their pace. His urgency unnerved her.

"You think I'm dealing drugs?" She blinked rapidly. A soft breeze sent leaves skittering across the sidewalk then up into the air, like a minicyclone, much like her thoughts.

"I never said that. The FBI has been tracking a package that's gone missing. We didn't know if the dealer got to it before we did or if it got misplaced. But after tonight, I think whoever shipped it is still looking for it."

Pinpricks of realization washed over her scalp and shoulders. "You're not in town to help your grandfather. You're here to investigate a drug deal."

"Yes." The single word came out clipped.

"And you didn't tell me because you think I'm

involved." Ellie hated the squeaky quality of her voice. "I'm not," she added out of desperation.

Johnny studied her a minute. "I believe you." His cool tone made her wonder if she believed *him*.

She cocked her head and was about to say as much but something stopped her. "What does this mean?"

Johnny huffed in frustration. "I'd feel better if we had this discussion someplace less out in the open."

"Tell me what it means." Ellie crossed her arms and stood there like a stubborn preteen determined to get her way.

"It means I'm investigating drug trafficking in Williamstown. There's some nasty stuff out there."

"So you slinked into town just like you did ten years ago, only this time you're an FBI agent and not a rookie cop."

He jerked his head back as if her words had hit their mark.

"One thing remains the same," she said, as the pounding of her heart filled her ears, "you're lying to people to *supposedly* solve a case."

Johnny hiked his chin, a determined look in his eyes. "I'm here because of the recent drug overdose. I couldn't come blazing into town with a sign on my back. I've been honest with you tonight and I trust you'll keep the reason I'm in town in confidence."

Ellie shook her head, not knowing what to think.

"Listen, Ellie, someone thinks you have their drugs and they're willing to break into your store and attack you to get them." Johnny pinned her with his dark gaze.

"I don't have the package." She lifted a shaky hand and hugged the strap of her purse closer to her body.

"They don't know that."

The wind whipped up and rattled the branches of the trees, sending shadows dancing on the sidewalk under the street lamp. Ellie sniffed the air. *Rain.* She looked up at the starless sky. She pulled on the sleeves of her sweater and tucked her hands inside. As warm as it was during the day, the evenings tended to cool down quickly. That's how it was in early autumn in Western New York.

"Are you cold?" Johnny asked.

"Yes, and more than a little freaked."

Ellie quickened her pace, suddenly in agreement with Johnny's need to get her home. "Maybe the attack was just some kid fooling around. They've had trouble with kids and graffiti at the old mill. I read something about it in the paper," she added after he gave her a quizzical look.

"Maybe he wanted to grab some of my paint and I got in the way."

"I don't think that's the case." Johnny's matter-of-fact tone made her inexplicably angry.

Truth be told, neither did she. The intruder had asked about a package.

They turned up her driveway and Ellie slowed, her headache worsening. "You're not helping your grandfather get the house on Treehaven ready to sell?"

"I hope to convince my grandfather it's time to downsize. The house is too big for him. But he's reluctant. Mostly, it's a cover to allow me to conduct the investigation without drawing suspicion."

Ellie felt the right thing to do would be to thank him for his honesty, but after their history, she couldn't muster the words.

"I live in the apartment over the garage," Ellie said instead, scanning her surroundings. Neat homes set back from the street with lots of shrubbery. Shrubbery an attacker could hide behind.

A band of fear tightened around her chest, making it difficult to breathe.

Thin lines of stress accented Johnny's eyes. "Lock the doors. I'll give Officer Bailey a call. Couldn't hurt to have extra patrols in your neighborhood."

Ellie made an awkward sound; a cross between disbelief and fear.

Johnny touched her hand. "Whoever attacked you tonight was pretty clumsy. They also made a rookie mistake using a national shipping company to transport illegal drugs. Every indication points to a low-level drug dealer who's stumbling around."

"So, you don't think he'll come and kill me in my bed?" She forced a smile and a strangled laugh sounded on her lips.

The dark shadow on his face made his expression difficult to read, but she sensed a smile. "I'll make sure that doesn't happen."

Warmth crept up her neck. She didn't want to ask him how he intended to do that.

"Instead of staying in the garage apartment, maybe you could stay in the main house?" Johnny spoke in the way a person does when they're constantly assessing the situation, trying to figure out what's best.

"Ha! And tell my mother, who already thinks the gift shop is not a fiscally sound idea, that I was attacked in the back room the night before I even opened?" And moving back into her old room would send her plans of independence back to step zero. Living above the garage was bad enough.

"I'll take that as a no."

"You said it was some rookie stumbling

around…" She knew she was grasping at any assurances he threw her way.

"Rookie criminals get desperate, too. Especially if they think you have something that's theirs."

"I don't." Ellie's shoulders slumped in frustration.

"They don't know that. I'm afraid you won't be safe as long as they think you do."

TWO

"Well…" Ellie sighed heavily "…today didn't go as I'd planned." She dragged a hand down the length of her ponytail and rested her elbow on the railing of the stairs leading to her apartment above the garage. She wasn't quite ready to call it a night. She'd never be able to sleep now. But she couldn't very well invite him in for coffee. Johnny wasn't exactly her friend, even if he had come to her rescue tonight.

Inwardly she bristled at the notion. She was not going to continue her trend of letting men rescue her. She could stand on her own two feet.

Johnny cleared his throat. "How are your parents?"

A small part of Ellie was relieved that Johnny wasn't ready to call it a night, either.

"Dad's been gone three years." The back of her nose prickled. "Good thing, too, because if he saw you standing in his driveway, he'd come out here and knock you into next week." She laughed at the memory of her high-spirited father cursing Johnny Rock up and down for tricking his son into this "whole drug business" as he'd called it.

"I'm sorry. I didn't know." There was something about his deep voice, his offer of sympathy in the cover of darkness, that felt more personal than it was. She didn't know Johnny. Not really.

How could someone make a living pretending he was something he wasn't and in the process mess up an innocent boy's future? Johnny should have been more careful with his accusations.

"I'm sure he would be proud of you," Johnny added.

Ellie shifted her stance. "I like to think so, but sometimes I don't know. I used to say I wanted to go to college to study art. He'd tell me to be an art teacher. He was always practical. Not sure he'd like the idea of a gift shop."

"Did you study art in college?"

Ellie's stomach dropped at the mention of college.

A fat raindrop landed on her cheek and she wiped it away. "After my parents paid for my brother's high-priced lawyer, there was no money left for college. For either of us."

"I'm sorry things worked out that way."

A few more drops plopped onto her head and

shoulders and sounded loudly on the metal trash cans near the garage.

"But you're not sorry for having my brother arrested?"

"We could go round and round about this until we're both soaking wet." Johnny squinted up at the sky.

She shook her head. "I better get inside." Another drop fell, then another and another.

Oh, just great.

Ellie grabbed Johnny's arm and pulled him toward her mother's front porch. She wasn't about to invite him into her apartment. "Wait out the storm. You'll get soaked."

The porch light flipped on and her mother appeared in the doorway.

Even greater.

Inwardly, Ellie rolled her eyes. Her mother was going to blow a gasket when she saw Johnny Rock standing on her porch with her daughter.

Nancy Winters squinted and tented a hand over her eyes to shield them from the bare bulb on the overhang of the front porch. "Hello, Ellie. Who do you have there?" A hint of accusation laced her mother's tone. The screen door creaked as her mother pushed it open with an outstretched arm.

Before she had a chance to answer, Johnny smiled and extended his hand. "Hello, Mrs.

Winters. It's Johnny… Johnny Rock. It's nice to see you."

An expression Ellie had seen a million times settled on her mother's features. The I'm-angry-but-it-will-have-to-wait look. The look her mother whipped out in the presence of company. "Hello, Johnny." Her brow furrowed. "Is everything okay?"

"Johnny ran into me on Main Street. He offered to walk me home." The words tumbled out of Ellie's mouth.

Her mother glanced at the overhang as the rain poured down. "Come in out of the weather. The rain will still get you if the wind starts up."

Johnny raised his hand, about to protest. Ellie shook her head slightly. "You might as well come in. My mom won't take no for an answer."

He shrugged and smiled. He had grown more handsome in the ten years since she had seen him. His brown hair was cut close on the sides and a little longer on top. Hair a girl could run her fingers through.

Where did that come from?

A smile curved his mouth and heat warmed her cheeks. Good thing he couldn't read minds.

"I suppose I'll come in," he said, "until the rain lets up."

Ellie held the door and Johnny brushed past her. His clean scent tickled her nose and a fondness coiled around her heart. Oh, she didn't need this complication in her life.

Johnny glanced down at her and she smiled tightly at him, dismissing her feelings as remnants of a silly schoolgirl crush.

"Have a seat," Ellie said, holding her hand out toward the small kitchen table in front of the windows. Johnny did as she said. Ellie took the chair across from him, fully aware of his masculine presence in the small space.

Why couldn't the rain have held off for five more minutes?

"So, what brings you here, Johnny?" Her mother busied herself filling the teakettle at the kitchen sink.

Ellie shot Johnny a don't-mention-the-intruder look.

"My grandfather is selling the house on Tree-haven Road. I'm giving him a hand organizing and packing. That sort of thing."

Nancy set the kettle on the stove with a deliberate clunk. She turned the back burner to high and set about the business of getting out three teacups and the tea bags before bothering to ask if they wanted any tea. A rainy evening called for tea, whether they agreed or not.

"And you're able to get away from your job?" Her mother crossed her arms and glared at him;

a searing look that would have had the teenage Ellie confessing to sins she hadn't committed.

"I'll be following up on some work-related things while I'm here. I work for the FBI." Johnny hooked his arm around the back of the chair, oblivious to the tension hovering in the air. Ellie imagined FBI agents didn't spook easily.

"You're with the FBI now, huh?" Her mother seemed to be considering something as she tore the paper away from the tea bag.

"Yes, ma'am. In Buffalo."

Nancy's features softened as if she had come to some conclusion. "Johnny, did you hear Greg has a good job working for the town? He's in maintenance. Makes good money working overtime. Good benefits."

"Good to hear."

"And Ellie is opening a shop in town—but you probably know that, too." Her mother stood tall, like a proud mama bear ready to swipe at anyone who dared hurt her cubs.

"Mom…" Ellie hated how her tone made her sound juvenile. Far younger than her twenty-four years.

Ellie swallowed the bile rising in her throat. She wondered why God would send rain when she was seconds away from getting rid of Johnny and her mother being none the wiser.

"How did you run into Ellie tonight?"

Ellie shot Johnny a sideways glance that didn't go unnoticed by her mother.

"What? What are you hiding from me?"

If Ellie could have melted into the floor like that wicked witch, she would have poured her hot tea over her head. No one lied to Nancy Winters. No one. The FBI had nothing on her mother's well-honed lie detector.

Ellie inhaled a deep breath and then let it spill. "Tonight when I was painting in the shop, I left the alley door propped open." A ticking started in her head. "Someone snuck in—"

"Snuck in!" Her mother's hand flew to her chest. "Did something happen to you? Are you hurt?" She rushed to Ellie's side and cupped her daughter's cheeks with her cool hands.

Suddenly feeling very conspicuous, Ellie pushed back in her chair and smiled awkwardly up at her mother. "I'm fine. Just a little paint in my hair and on my T-shirt." She swallowed around her fear. "You know how those teens have been doing graffiti on the stone walls at the park? Kids were probably looking to steal my paint and I surprised them."

She hoped God would forgive her this little white lie to spare her mother a sleepless night.

Nancy's worried eyes moved to Johnny. "Is that what happened?"

His gaze flicked to Ellie, then back to her mother.

"Officer Bailey is looking into it. I'll follow up with him if it'd make you feel better."

"Oh…I… I'm sure our local police are more than capable." Ellie's mother must have remembered she didn't want to ask the likes of Johnny for help.

Or perhaps her mother feared her daughter would get swept off her feet again. Make another stupid mistake. And with the man who had ruined her brother's life.

But what her mother had yet to realize: Ellie refused to get involved with anyone. She was done looking for approval through a man's eyes.

The next morning Johnny wandered down the back stairway into his grandfather's kitchen. Through the exterior French doors, he was surprised to see the eighty-year-old man raking leaves in the backyard, his golden retriever keeping him company. His grandfather was ten years older than when Johnny had moved in with him for his undercover narcotics position at the high school, and his face was thinner, but he still kept active. This old house was a lot to maintain.

However, a neighbor had caught Johnny in the driveway yesterday and expressed some concerns about his grandfather's physical ability. Johnny hadn't been around long enough to determine if this was a valid concern or simply the grumblings of a neighbor who didn't like that his grandfather's once stately Victorian had fallen into disrepair.

Johnny opened the doors to the outside and the crisp morning air hit him. He stepped down onto the stone patio. Dandelions pushed through the cracks between the pavers. Maybe he'd fix a few things while he was here. Every improvement would help his grandfather sell the place sooner—if only he could convince him now was the perfect time to sell.

To date Johnny hadn't been able to convince his grandfather of anything.

"You're up early," Johnny called to his grandfather.

His grandfather, or "Buddy" as most people called him, stopped raking and rested his elbow on the handle. "The older I get, the less I sleep."

Johnny imagined his grandfather had a lot of regrets that kept him awake at night.

"Any break in the case?"

Johnny bent and yanked a dandelion out by the roots. "Not yet." He had told his grandfather he was in town working on a case, but he hadn't given him many details. It wasn't that he didn't trust his grandfather; he just didn't want to put the elderly gentleman in the position of accidentally compromising an active investigation.

"Your investigation… Does it have anything to do with that intruder over at the new gift shop?"

Johnny angled his head and studied his grandfather. "How did you know about that?"

Duke, the golden retriever, ran over to Johnny and was rewarded with a pat on the head. Johnny pulled a dry leaf from the patch of gray in the dog's fur.

"Heard about it when I ran up to the convenience store for the morning paper."

"Nothing goes unnoticed in a small town."

"You should know that by now." Buddy arched his gray brow. "Whatever you're working on, be careful. People have long memories and still blame you for ruining those boys' lives."

"You mean the boys I arrested for dealing drugs at the high school?" Johnny bit back the sarcasm.

"One of them wasn't convicted."

"Doesn't mean he wasn't guilty."

"That's not how people think. You know that. People don't forget." His grandfather jabbed at a pile of leaves with the rake. "Sometimes I think more people were upset you ruined the chances of the baseball team going to the state championship than about the arrests themselves."

Johnny shook his head. "There's more at stake now. A young boy died of a drug overdose. I need to get these drugs off the street. They are nasty stuff. Deadlier than most."

His grandfather walked toward him and stumbled on a root. Johnny lunged forward to catch him, but the older man righted himself with the support of the rake before Johnny reached him. "Stupid roots." Buddy shook his head. "I know how important this investigation is. Even though there's plenty of crime in Buffalo, you keep ending up back here in Williamstown."

"The chief of police requested the FBI's help."

"Maybe after you reached out to them after seeing news of the boy's death on TV?" The sudden surge of deaths due to drugs throughout the area had made the death of a Williamstown honor student news, even forty minutes away in Buffalo.

Johnny didn't say anything.

His grandfather balanced the rake against a small patio table and lowered himself slowly onto a wrought-iron chair that could have used a fresh coat of paint. He rubbed Duke's head playfully and made a few affectionate noises. After a minute he said, "Your being here has nothing to do with Mary Claire getting hooked on drugs when she was a student at Williamstown?"

Buddy's hands shook as he spoke of his only daughter. Johnny's mother.

Johnny swallowed around a lump in his throat, not trusting his voice.

"You never did get over losing your mother."

How did one get over losing a mother due to a drug overdose when he was twelve, which had then landed him in foster care? No, that pretty much stuck in a kid's mind. Forever.

Johnny was lucky—if he could call it that—that he had just come off a pretty rough case and his direct supervisor at the FBI had thought he needed some downtime. They had agreed on a compromise: Johnny could take a pseudo leave of absence and help his grandfather get the old Victorian house ready for sale, all while serving in an official FBI capacity to help the Williamstown police department get the drugs off the street.

The wind whispered through the trees, sending more leaves floating to the ground. "You've got a big job out here," Johnny said, referring to the leaves.

Johnny didn't like talking about his mother, even though her loss was seldom far from his mind. His grandfather rarely mentioned her either, so this morning's comment had thrown Johnny for a loop. He and his grandfather had a cordial relationship. Not a deep one.

"You know I would have taken you in when you lost your mother if I could have." His grandfather glanced up at him briefly with glistening eyes, and then away to his faithful companion as if embarrassed. "See, your grandmother... Well, Dottie couldn't accept that her daughter... her only child, had made so many bad decisions."

Johnny had never understood why he'd had to go into foster care. Why his grandparents had never taken him in. When he'd tried to broach the topic years ago, Buddy had changed the subject. Perhaps when Johnny had come to stay with his grandfather a decade ago—a few months after his grandmother had died—he hadn't yet been ready to open up.

"I appreciate you letting me crash here now. That's what counts." Johnny struggled to get the words out without revealing emotion. He had gotten good at that over the years.

His grandfather had a distant look in his eyes. "I should have insisted we take you in when you were just a young boy. It wasn't right what we did to you." Regret rolled off him in waves and crashed on Johnny, pounding him with his own list of *shoulda-coulda-woulda*s. "Your grandmother was in so much pain and seeing you was a reminder of everything we had lost. I thought..."

Johnny put his hand on his grandfather's shoulder as if to say, "It's okay," since the words got clogged in his throat. He took a moment to compose himself. "As far as anyone else is concerned,

I'm in town to help you move. Only the local police are aware of the drug investigation."

And Ellie knew, but he didn't want to get into that yet with his grandfather. Part of him was glad she knew. He wanted to be honest with her. Not hide behind his usual cloak of some fake identity.

As long as she was deserving of his trust.

"I don't want to leave this old place. Where would I go?" The lost look in his grandfather's eyes cut through him. "And what about Duke?" Buddy patted the dog's back. "Maybe it's time you moved on, son. There's plenty of crime in Buffalo, right?" Buddy's mouth slanted into a sad, lopsided grin.

"Yes, I'm afraid there is. But I need to be here."

"I'm afraid we'll never find peace. No matter what. Mary Claire's death was senseless."

Johnny jerked his head back.

"Don't look at me like that. You know what I mean. You're trying to fix a wrong that can't be fixed."

"If I can save one kid, it'll be worth it."

"Make sure you don't lose yourself in the process." Buddy stood and approached Johnny. He tapped his grandson's cheek.

Nostalgia made his gut ache. He wished the years of hurt hadn't bent his grandfather's once-tall stature.

Johnny found himself studying the overgrown

tree roots pushing through the plush grass. "I have plans later this afternoon, but I thought we could start by going through the closets in the bedrooms this morning."

"I don't need you to be creating projects for me. I had had a lifetime of honey-do lists from Dottie." His grandfather gave him a hard smile and looked up at the large Victorian.

Johnny recalled his mother's grumbling about her childhood, always painting a far different picture. Johnny couldn't reconcile this beautiful home and his friendly grandfather with the dark childhood Mary Claire Rock had described. His mother had been an angry woman.

"I'm not ready to move. Your grandmother and I had so many hopes when we first moved in…" Buddy's voice trailed off. Not all their hopes had been realized.

"I know." That was only partially true. Johnny had no idea what it would be like to have roots so deep. Johnny had no idea what it meant to have roots at all. His mother had always kept them on the move. And foster care had added to his sense of instability.

Would any place ever feel like home?

Later that day at the grand opening of the gift shop, Ashley came up behind Ellie and cupped her shoulders.

Ashley whispered into her ear, "Are you looking for something?"

Ellie sucked in a quick breath, trying not to overreact to her friend's stealth approach from behind. *Doesn't she realize that that's the last thing you did to a person who had recently been attacked in this very same location?*

At this rate, Ellie was going to be terrified to enter the storage room of her gift shop.

Heart racing in her ears, Ellie glanced down to see a stuffed mushroom with a bite out of it pinched between Ashley's expensively manicured fingertips. The offending food hovered inches away from the sleeve on Ellie's new pink dress. A definite splurge for a poor, new business owner.

Ellie pivoted away and forced a smile. She grabbed a towel off the edge of the sink and dried her hands. "Thanks for unpacking these boxes." She figured that was better than asking her friend why she couldn't have taken the time to collapse the boxes for recycling. "How much longer did you work this afternoon after I left?"

Ashley frowned and seemed to notice for the first time the boxes discarded in an unorganized heap in the corner.

Ellie noted the shadow darkening the surface of her friend's eyes; a confused look she had perfected when she either didn't want to give an answer or when she truly didn't know the answer.

Ashley popped the stuffed mushroom into her mouth and blinked a few times. "I didn't unpack those boxes," she said around a mouthful. She peeked into one of the open boxes. "They're not empty. Maybe you started to unpack them and forgot in your whirlwind."

Had she? Ellie fiddled with her bracelet. It didn't seem likely. She might be frazzled, but forgetful?

"Did you lock the door when you left? Set the alarm?" Ellie knew she shouldn't have left before Ashley, but her friend had insisted on waiting for Tony and Ellie'd had a hair appointment she hadn't wanted to be late to.

Ellie tried not to let her mind jump to the worst possible scenario. *Was someone searching for something?* She was determined to control her rioting emotions. A few guests had already filtered into the shop. She shouldn't be wasting time in the storage room. She had only run back here to wash her hands.

"Of course, I locked the door." Ashley shrugged, sweeping her long blond hair over one shoulder and combing her fingers through it much like a person holding a kitten and stroking its fur. Ashley had done this for as long as Ellie could remember: first with a long braid in kindergarten and then with her smooth, flat-ironed locks in high school.

"And the alarm?" Ellie frantically searched her memory. She had been too stressed and distracted when she'd arrived at the shop this evening to remember if she had turned off the alarm or not.

Ashley shrugged again. "Not the alarm." She waved her hand in a dismissive gesture. "It was the middle of the day." One corner of her mouth turned up. "What? You think someone broke in here and messed up a few boxes?"

"I told you what happened last night. Someone—" she lowered her voice into a harsh whisper "—attacked me. Right here." She jabbed her index finger at the stain of orange paint on the floor. She had left out the part about Johnny's investigation.

A contrite expression settled on Ashley's features. "I'll make sure I set the alarm from now on." She adjusted the belt on her dress. "But you and I know we were so busy this morning making final preparations that we might have knocked those boxes over. Who knows?" Ashley gently tapped Ellie's forehead. "Don't let your overactive imagination get the best of you."

Ellie rolled her shoulders, trying to ease the tension. "Maybe you're right." The haphazard pile of boxes taunted her.

"I came back here to tell you your handsome FBI guy has arrived."

"Really? Johnny's here?" She smoothed a hand

down the front of her dress and Ashley lifted a knowing eyebrow.

Ellie was already regretting that she had mentioned that Johnny had happened by last night after the attack. Ashley was duly impressed that he was an FBI agent. And her singsong tone when she announced his arrival indicated she'd never let Ellie forget she had once had a schoolgirl crush on him. Ashley had witnessed firsthand how Ellie would linger in the family room when her brother would have his friends over to watch a baseball game on TV. Her skin heated with the memory. Ellie had made such a fool of herself mooning over her brother's friend.

Ellie opened her mouth to tell her that Johnny wasn't *her* handsome FBI guy, but decided protesting at a moment like this would be a tactical error. Protesting would be a huge flag for Ashley to hoist and run with, broadcasting everything Ashley knew about her friend's crush. Well…before Johnny had turned out to be an undercover narcotics officer.

"Well, aren't you going to greet him?" The single question was rife with expectation.

"We better get out front and see to *all* of our guests," Ellie said, deflecting her friend's line of questioning. They slowed in the doorway and she whispered, "Looks like a great turnout."

"Of course. Did you expect any less?" Ashley leaned in close, smelling of garlic and feta and a hint of olive oil. "Now, you better go talk to that yummy man over there or I will." She leaned in close to Ellie and pointed slyly with a hooked index finger at Johnny who was studying a painting on the wall.

One of her paintings.

Perhaps sensing their eyes on him, he turned and faced her, a wide smile splitting his handsome face. She felt her face flush. *Again.* She glanced away so as not to be caught staring. Man, Johnny looked sharp in a casual sport coat and collared shirt.

"You sure got it bad," Ashley said and laughed. All the reasons Ellie was drawn to Ashley were displayed on her friend's playful expression. Ashley saw the bright side in everything. Nothing got her down. Ashley tapped her friend's arm and waggled her eyebrows before strolling away to greet some other guests.

Ellie shook off her misgivings about the upended open boxes in the storage room and walked over to greet Johnny.

"The store looks great," he said. "You got the shelves on the back wall up."

The shelving unit softened the bold color she had been second-guessing from the minute she had opened the paint can. "Thanks. I'm happy with how it turned out." She rubbed the back of her neck. "How did you know about the grand opening?"

He studied her, a hint of amusement on his face. "The flyer on the front window."

"Oh," she said, suddenly feeling foolish. "Of course."

Johnny pointed to the painting on the wall that he had been studying. "You're talented."

"I was inspired." Tucking a strand of hair behind her ear, she dipped her head. She had never learned to take a compliment. On the canvas, she had captured the sun exploding over the horizon, the purple and pink clouds floating over the ocean. Looking at God's creation even now filled her with awe.

Standing close to Johnny, she noticed that tiny lines etched the corners of his eyes, reflecting the ten years since she had last seen him. She also detected a hint of aloe aftershave and Dove soap and smiled to herself. That's how he'd smelled back when he used to hang out at her house, sitting around the table with her family.

Almost part of the family. That's why his accusations had hurt so much.

"Everything okay?" Johnny asked, snapping her out of her reverie.

"Yeah, I think so."

"Are your brother and mom here?" The small shop was crowded.

"Unfortunately my niece Grace is in the talent show at school. I had already advertised the grand opening in the paper, so I couldn't switch nights." Ellie shrugged, but couldn't deny the disappointment that had settled in her gut. Perhaps it was better this way. Her mother thought her efforts were a waste of time and money.

"That's too bad."

"Yeah, but I'd hate for Grace to be disappointed." She rubbed her bare arm, eager to change the subject. "Some opened boxes were knocked over in the back this afternoon. Can't say for sure if they were like that before I left to get ready for the party."

"But you don't think they were?"

Ellie bit her lip. "I'm pretty organized. Ashley, on the other hand…and she was the last to leave."

"I'll wander back there and check it out."

The chimes on the door jangled and a few more guests filled the small space.

"Did you or the police find out anything more about last night?" she whispered.

Johnny shook his head. "Sorry."

The celebratory mood had deflated as her nerves buzzed at the memory of being attacked yesterday.

"Enough of that." He gestured with his head toward the food. "Those appetizers look great. Any chance you have those little hot-dog thingies wrapped in crescent rolls?"

Ellie felt a smile pulling at her lips. "No, I must have left those off the menu."

His forehead crinkled. "Really?"

"No, not really." She laughed. "I was shooting for a little more upscale."

Johnny adjusted the flap of his sport coat. "Are you saying I'm not upscale?"

"I enjoy a hot dog as much as the next guy, but tonight is more a scallop-wrapped-in-bacon kinda night."

"Bacon?" Humor lit Johnny's brown eyes. "You are definitely my kind of girl."

Ellie felt like that fourteen-year-old girl with a crush on her brother's best friend. She was *so* in trouble.

No, no, no. She was not looking for a relationship. Based on the last one, she was horrible at judging men. She was determined to make a go of it alone. And the easiest solution? No more relationships.

The door bells chimed in the background, saving Ellie from making a fool of herself. She patted Johnny's arm. "Go find yourself some bacon. I need to greet my guests."

She felt Johnny's eyes on her as she walked away. She plastered on a smile and greeted members from her church and the neighborhood. She hoped tonight's success was an indication of the shop's future.

A few times over the course of the evening,

she found Johnny watching her and she wondered if he was here to protect her or because he thought she was somehow involved with this so-called missing package. Or maybe he just really liked her bacon-wrapped appetizers. Ellie really didn't want to believe he was suspicious of her, but Johnny *had* crushed her family when he'd had her brother arrested for dealing drugs. He had insinuated himself into her family's lives to suit his purposes. Was he getting close to her for reasons all his own?

She shook away the thought. She'd keep her distance. She had no interest in a relationship, genuine or otherwise. But definitely not otherwise.

And she did feel better with him around. He did carry a gun, after all, and someone seemed to have a beef with her.

The bells on the door jangled and the last guest left. Ashley had departed a few minutes earlier, ducking out with her new boyfriend Tony. She had promised to come back early tomorrow morning to help clean up, but Ashley knew Ellie well enough to know she couldn't lock the door without cleaning up.

Ellie tossed a few empty food trays into the garbage.

Johnny gathered up some cups scattered around the shop.

"Thank you, but you really don't need to help."

"I don't mind."

Ellie was about to say something then decided to let it rest. Even though a million thoughts ping-ponged around her head, she didn't need to share them all with Johnny.

A crash sounded from the back of the store and Ellie jumped, splashing the contents of the punch bowl up and over the edge. Her mind flashed to last night: the man slamming her body against the utility sink; his calloused hand against her mouth. She gasped, a cold fear washing over her.

Johnny moved toward her, a concerned look on his face. He held out his hand, indicating she stay put.

Ellie swallowed hard as she watched him disappear into the storage room, her pulse beating erratically in her ears. A few minutes later he returned with a piece of paper. He locked gazes with Ellie.

Her stomach dropped.

"This was stuffed in the hole of a brick." He pointed with his thumb toward the back door. "There's a nice dent in the middle of the exterior door where he threw the brick."

Tiny stars danced in Ellie's line of vision. "What does it say?" The words rasped out of her dry throat.

She read over his shoulder. In angry black letters, the wrinkled note read, "Stop playing games or you die."

THREE

Ellie worked a long shift at the gift shop the next day. Ashley had popped in for a bit—safety in numbers and all—but she'd scooted out shortly after Tony had called midway through the day. Ashley was about as reliable as cell service five minutes outside of town. Ellie knew she couldn't count on either.

Wrapping up the day, Ellie did some final bookkeeping and waited for Johnny to escort her home, as they'd arranged after the appearance of the threatening note last night. As soon as business hours were over, she had locked both the front and back doors to her shop. Rolling her shoulders, she blinked her eyes slowly. She hated that the very thing she had dreamed would make her feel independent was making her feel like a prisoner.

The sun hung low on the horizon and soon it would be dark. The fine hairs on the back of her neck stood on edge.

Was someone out there watching her? Thinking she had stolen a package of drugs?

She sent up a silent prayer of protection. And patience.

Ellie didn't want to fail at yet something else in her life. She had thought following her boyfriend to Buffalo was her ticket out of sleepy Williamstown, but it had only ended in heartache. He was more interested in controlling her than in letting her follow her dreams. Never again would she get herself in that trap.

She picked up her pen and added some figures at the bottom of the ledger. She preferred paper to a computer program. At this rate, the shop would barely break even.

Don't get ahead of yourself, it's only the first full day.

She scratched her head with the bottom of the pen and frowned. Ellie would have to find a way to attract more customers.

A banging at the front door made her drop the pen. Pinpricks of panic shot up her arms and she gasped. Framed through the glass of the front door was Bobby Vino, the baker from next door. Tony's father. His chubby face was contorted into a very angry expression.

"What now?" Ellie muttered to herself as she strolled to the front door. Five more minutes and she would have been gone for the night and could have avoided whatever she was about to face.

Lately, her life had boiled down to bad timing.

She squared her shoulders and opened the door. "Hello, Mr. Vino. Is something wrong?"

His face glowed red. "Your stupid shop cost me a very important customer."

She clasped her hands in front of her. "I'm sorry. I don't understand." Behind Mr. Vino, she noticed his son Tony approaching, the blank expression on his face not giving her any indication as to whose side he was on. In the far reaches of her brain she was wondering why Ashley had left the shop so early if her date was still working. She quickly dismissed the thought, instead plastering on her most sympathetic face.

Mr. Vino jerked his thumb toward the street. "Your customers last night took up all the convenient parking spots on Main Street. My customer couldn't get in to order a cake for her daughter's birthday."

Ellie blinked rapidly. "That hardly seems worthy of getting this fired up over."

Tony stepped forward and placed a hand on his father's shoulder. "The person has been one of our longtime customers. My father fears if he's lost her, how many others has he lost."

"I'm sorry that happened." Ellie thought about the trickle of customers today. "I don't think parking will be an issue in the future." Unfortunately for her bottom line.

Mr. Vino's jowls wobbled as he shook his head, the anger rolling off him in waves. "Another person thinking she has what it takes to run a successful business, but doesn't have a clue."

Ellie opened her mouth to sling an angry insult. *How dare he?* He didn't even know her. But her father's wisdom whispered across her brain, "You'll catch more flies with honey than with vinegar."

"You should have never leased this space." Mr. Vino smacked his son's hand off his shoulder, spun on his white-cushioned shoes and stormed out of her shop and back into his own.

"Wow." Ellie took a step back. "Your father is a very angry man."

Tony pulled off the hat covering his hair, crumpled it in his fist and smiled at her a little sheepishly. "Sorry about my dad. He's really a nice guy when he isn't stressed."

Ellie crossed her arms. "We're all stressed. But I learned a long time ago, we can't control what other people do."

"Is Ashley here?" Tony asked.

"She left a while ago." Ellie strolled back over to her paperwork, not in the mood for small talk. "I thought she was with you."

"Oh." Tony smoothed out his white hat in his

hands. "We're going out a little later." Tony approached the counter with an air of contrition. "Maybe if you understood where my dad is coming from."

Ellie looked up from her paperwork, but didn't say anything.

"My dad had hoped to rent this space and expand the business."

Ellie set her pen down. "I didn't realize…"

"Yeah, well…business has been slow. He thought an expansion might mean increased sales." Tony scratched the crown of his head, leaving a tuft of hair sticking up. "Then you moved in here and the customers from your grand opening blocked his parking spots." A vein throbbed in his forehead. "Then when he called one of his regulars about ordering her daughter's cake and he learned she had ordered it elsewhere. Well… he lost it."

Ellie held out her hand. "Like I said, no need to fight over parking spots now." An unease shifted in her gut. She hoped this wasn't a sign of things to come.

"The old man's gotten a little more grumpy." Tony stuffed his hat into the back pocket of his jeans and shifted his stance. "I hope we can be good neighbors. My dad's worked hard all his life. He's a good guy."

"I'm sure he is."

Tony whistled under his breath and strolled around the perimeter of the small store, his rubber soles sounding quietly on the wood floor. For the first time she noticed his orange-and-yellow sneakers, something one of the kids in the church youth group would wear. She held back a smile.

Tony stopped near the door to the storage room and his forehead furrowed, as if he had suddenly remembered something. "Has the FBI agent figured out any more about the guy that attacked you?"

Ellie studied Tony's face. "You know about the attack?"

"I work next door," he said, his expression neutral.

"Not yet," she said, leaving it at that. She wasn't sure if she detected neighborly concern or plain curiosity. He did have a shop next door and a right to know.

Tony nodded slowly, as if considering this. He had a tired mannerism about him. His hands clenched briefly before he seemed to relax. "How well do you know Johnny Rock?"

"Not very." Which was the truth. The boy she had had a teenage crush on had been playing a role. He hadn't been a teen at all. Yet she couldn't deny the immediate sense of attraction, then and now. She blinked a few times. What did fourteen-year-olds know anyway?

"Does Johnny think the attack was random?"

Tingling unease bit at her fingertips. *What's with all the questions?* "They're investigating."

"The FBI? Or the local police?"

"Both, I guess."

Tony shrugged. "Probably some kids."

"Maybe." Ellie studied him careful.

Tony laughed, a mirthless sound, and leaned his shoulder against the door frame of the storage room. "It's been awhile since you've lived in a small town. People talk."

"And…"

"Everyone is talking about how Johnny's back and looking for the dealer who sold that poor kid some bad stuff that got him killed."

"You say that like it's a bad thing." She planted a fist on her hip.

"So, it's true?"

Ellie dropped her fist from her hip and picked up her pencil distractedly. She shook her head. "I wouldn't know." Heat fired in her face as she glared down at her ledger. She was a horrible liar. But she had no choice. Johnny had asked for discretion. A serious investigation was at stake.

"It just seems coincidental that Johnny would show up out of the blue after that kid overdosed." The lines on Tony's face smoothed and something flitted in the depths of his eyes. "I was a freshman in high school back when all those arrests were made. I still remember the day the local cops came into the school with drug-sniffing dogs."

Tony pushed off the wall and stared at her coolly. "Why am I telling you? Your brother was one of them."

The way he said "one of them" made icy water flow through her veins. "My brother wasn't convicted."

"The accusations messed him up all the same." *More than you know.*

"I suppose not as bad as Roger Petersen who served time in prison for his part." In a way, Ellie felt as if she needed to defend Johnny. Although her innocent brother had gotten caught up in the mess, a young man *had* gone to prison for distributing drugs. He had been convicted, right? Even if he had proclaimed his innocence.

Roger had moved around for a while before moving back to Williamstown last year. He seemed to be making a go of it. He had a new wife and had opened a sub shop two blocks away on Main Street. For some crazy reason, Greg and he had rekindled their friendship.

"People make mistakes." She was referring to Roger, but something in Tony's expression made her suspect he thought she was talking about Johnny. She let it go. "People deserve to be forgiven."

"I'm all about forgiveness," Tony said. "But don't forget, Johnny used people to get what he wanted."

Ellie stared blankly at Tony, waiting for him to make his point.

"He got close to your brother. Close to all the guys on the high school baseball team to get what he needed."

She rubbed the back of her neck. "He needed to get drugs off the street."

Tony leaned in conspiratorially. "True, but he did it in a way that destroyed innocent people's lives. In return, he got a nice promotion and then eventually a pretty nice job with the FBI."

Hadn't she worried about the same things?

The threat of a headache thumped behind her eyes.

"Listen, I don't mean to be a drag. Ashley and I are getting close and I know she loves you like a sister. I'd hate for this guy to hurt you because he's using you." He lifted his palm. "You know, like a means to an end?"

The numbers on her ledger swirled and she blinked rapidly to clear her vision.

Tony strolled toward the exit and put his hand on the silver bar on the door. "Doesn't matter. I was just making small talk." He paused longer than necessary. "Again, I'm sorry about my dad. If you have any more problems, come see me. He's under a lot of stress to pay the bills. I'm trying to convince him to expand with internet sales, but he's old school." He gave his head a small shake. "Maybe it's time to close up shop."

Alarm shot through Ellie's veins. "You can't be serious?" An empty shop next to hers would be the kiss of death. The bakery attracted more customers onto Main Street. Fewer businesses, less traffic.

Tony shrugged. "My father wouldn't go quietly. That's for sure. His grandfather opened this bakery in 1927."

Ellie stood dumbfounded as Tony walked out of the store. She tapped her pen absentmindedly on the counter. She couldn't worry about Tony's family business. She had a business of her own to worry about. But what haunted her were Tony's questions about Johnny.

Would Johnny use her to get what he needed?

No, he was protecting her.

Or maybe he was doing a bit of both. Johnny had been known to do whatever he needed to do to get the job done. Even if it meant destroying innocent people.

Johnny had split his day between helping his reluctant grandfather sort through some of the items in his house and fielding calls from an FBI agent in the home office in Buffalo. The FBI had made a big arrest at the Canadian border a short drive north of Williamstown, but Johnny knew the war on drugs was like plugging a leak on a sinking rowboat while another leak sprung up. You could keep paddling, you might get closer to the shore, but soon you'd be underwater all the same.

Someone in Williamstown was definitely supplying the hard-core stuff and Johnny was going to stop them before another kid got hooked or worse. He had to work his way back into the good graces of the residents in hopes of uncovering some leads. Sure, he heard the grumblings of some of the regulars at the diner. They seemed to focus on Greg Winters who'd gone free and not Roger Petersen who'd gone to prison. What people thought wasn't his problem. He had a job to do.

Johnny took his grandfather's golden retriever with him when he walked up to Gifts and More to escort Ellie home. He wished she'd just shut down the shop and leave town, but he knew that wasn't realistic. She was pretty stubborn. And so was he.

When he reached her block, he noticed the bakery next door was dark. At her door, the lights glowed, but he didn't see any sign of her.

He pulled on the door handle. *Locked.*

"Good girl," he muttered. Duke looked up at

him and then went back to sniffing around the nearby tree.

Ellie's auburn hair became visible over the surface of the counter. A second later she popped up. Concern slanted her mouth down at the corners and a crease lined her forehead. She set her purse by the register and strode toward the door. She was staring right at him, but the expression on her face was hard to read. The bolt snapped and then the door opened.

Ellie looked as though she wanted to yell at him when the dog caught her attention. She glanced at Johnny, the pinched expression around her eyes softening a bit. She crouched and took the dog's snout in her hands. "Hey, puppy." She straightened and brushed something off the thighs of her jeans. "Give me a minute while I close a few things up."

"I'll wait here with Duke. I'm afraid he'd be like the proverbial bull in a china shop."

"Ha." Ellie stepped back into the shop and went behind the register. Johnny kept the glass door propped open with his shoulder.

"How was business today?" he asked, glancing over his shoulder at the quiet street.

"Slow." The frustration was evident in her voice. "I'm going to have to think of something else to draw customers in." She paused, leaning the flat of her hand on the counter. "What do you think of those shops that hold art classes?" She shoved something under the counter. "Not art classes per se, but art parties. Women gather on a girls' night out, have refreshments and create artwork? Maybe even kids' birthday parties?"

"Never heard of them. Sounds like an interesting idea. With your artistic talent, it would definitely be something to consider."

Ellie walked to the door. "Maybe I could clear a space out near the back of the store for easels." She shrugged. "I still have a lot of thinking to do."

"You should." He reached down by his side and patted Duke's head.

She gave him a quizzical look. "You don't think it's stupid?" She said it in a way that made him think someone had put her down in the past. A lot.

"You're a smart lady. You'll figure it out." He threaded the leash through his hand. "If there's any help you need from me, let me know."

"Like a bodyguard?" The hopeful expression died in her eyes.

"Well, I hope that's only temporary." He didn't want to mention the dead end the FBI office had told him about today. Turned out the images from the security camera at the parcel service where the drugs had originated had been too grainy. Even when they enhanced them, the images were still unclear: a dark blob, perhaps a man wearing sunglasses and a hoodie. Not much to go on.

Ellie held up her finger and jogged back over to the counter to grab her purse. "Once you figure out who's been dealing drugs, you're out of here. Back to Buffalo."

"Buffalo's not that far." He couldn't help but smile at her. She had such a cynical look on her face. He tilted his head. "What's wrong? You seem annoyed." Maybe it was just a rough business day on top of everything else.

A look of hesitation lit her eyes. Her pink lips formed a straight line as if she were trying to find the words.

Johnny narrowed his gaze. "Did something happen today that you're not telling me?" His pulse spiked and he stepped into the store to get closer to her, but, in the excitement, Duke wagged his tail. A crystal unicorn wobbled on the glass shelf near the door. He reached out and steadied it before taking a step back toward the door. Duke wasn't helping here.

"I had a visitor today who suggested you might be using me for your investigation."

The defeated look on her face made his heart sink. "You told someone about the drug investigation?"

Her cheeks fired red. "No, not at all. But Tony

Vino next door was asking a lot of questions. He seems to think that's why you're in town."

"Interesting." He made a mental note.

"So, are you?"

"Using you?" He scratched his jaw. "You do realize you're smack-dab in the middle of whatever's going on here."

She crossed her arms and glared at him. "Not by choice."

"I know that. But someone thinks you intercepted a package of drugs. You're involved whether you like it or not. And it's my job to protect you."

"I know it's your *job*." Something about the way she stressed the word disappointed him. He had hopes that their relationship could grow into something more.

Johnny stepped forward again and the tug on the leash reminded him why he had remained in the doorway. "I thought we were friends."

"My brother thought you were his friend, too."

A muscle ticked in his jaw. If only he could share everything—the entire truth—with her.

"Are you saying I shouldn't protect you? You're in danger."

She bowed her head and her words lost their sharpness. "Someone has to get these horrible drug dealers off the street. I know that." She dropped her arms to her sides then clasped her hands in front of her.

Something about this reminded him of the fourteen-year-old girl he had met all those years ago. "What's on your mind?"

In the distance a siren wailed. Duke's ears perked up.

"I don't like to be lied to…or used," Ellie whispered as if the words were hard to say.

"I would never—"

Duke sprang to his feet and tugged on his leash. Johnny yanked it back. A police car and then an ambulance raced by the shop, filling the quiet night with their relentless wails. Johnny tilted his head. "I wonder what's going on."

Ellie stepped closer to him in the doorway to glance down the street after the vehicles. "I hope no one's hurt." A soft breeze blew a strand of hair across her face and he resisted the urge to sweep it aside. The flowery scent of her shampoo would stick with him for a while.

Ellie flipped off the lights and glanced around the shop one last time before locking it up for the night.

"Ellie—" Johnny lowered his voice "—I would never intentionally hurt you."

Ellie hiked a shoulder, as if she didn't really care. Or maybe because she didn't fully believe him. Why should she?

"Sounds like this Tony guy is trying to stir up problems where none exist." Johnny yanked on Duke's leash as the retriever tried to chase a dry leaf scraping across the concrete.

"That's not exactly true." Ellie pulled the glass door closed and fished around in her purse for the keys to lock it.

Johnny smiled, considering their complicated past. "Your brother?"

She nodded and looked up. The light from the lamppost glistened in her eyes.

Johnny hadn't been wrong about her brother. Greg was as guilty as Roger, but Greg had the better lawyer. *But why would Ellie ever believe me?* She loved her brother.

"Do what you need to do to bring these guys to justice, but please don't use me. I'm not involved with this package. No way. I promise you."

He stared at her for a minute. A million emotions flickered in her trusting eyes.

"Why do you think Tony was asking so many questions?" Johnny asked.

"It's a small town. People talk."

A loud engine from a motorcycle roared down the street, attracting his attention. Duke barked frantically at the ear-piercing sound, nearly wrenching Johnny's arm out of its socket.

The motorcycle slowed. A black helmet and dark shield masked the rider's identity. In the heavy shadows, the rider slowly lifted his hand. A long object came into focus.

A gun!

Johnny shoved Ellie back into the shop, pushing her down, covering her with his body, bringing Duke with them.

A whimpering Duke cowered inside the door. A high-pitched zing was barely discernible above the motorcycle's roar.

Glass from the shattered door rained down on them.

Ellie screamed.

FOUR

Ellie's feet went out from under her as Johnny used his body as a shield, pushing her down. She winced and braced for a jarring impact, but Johnny's hand under the back of her head softened the fall. She tried unsuccessfully to fill her lungs under his weight. Terror made her scalp prickle.

Were those shots? Had they just been shot at?

Her head spun. She couldn't think straight. This was surreal. Through a foggy, panic-induced tunnel, she could hear a dog barking frantically. The stillness of the moment sent icy fear coursing through her.

The calm after the storm.

"Johnny? Johnny, are you all right?" Ellie's words came out in a breathless rush. She reached up and touched his wet sleeve, red with blood. She swallowed around a knot in her throat.

Johnny shifted his weight off her and while still on the floor, glanced over his shoulder toward the street. He grimaced. From her vantage point, all she could see was the streetlight illuminating the three empty parking spots in front of her store. There was no visible street traffic save for the distant rumble of the departing motorcycle.

In one quick motion Johnny got to his feet in a hunched position, grabbed her arm and brought her to her feet. "Stay low." A subdued Duke followed them, as if the animal sensed the gravity of the situation. Johnny guided them toward the storage room and slammed the door shut and locked it.

He checked the exterior door leading to the alley before directing Ellie to the lone wooden chair in the corner of the room. She was about to protest, to tell him it was an expensive antique, but under the circumstances that seemed silly. Duke sat next to her and put his snout on her thigh, as if they were long-lost friends who had just shared a harrowing experience.

Johnny patted Duke's head. "Good boy. Everything's going to be all right." He was talking to the golden retriever, but his warm brown eyes were locked on Ellie's. He plucked his cell phone out of his belt.

She reached up and touched his arm. "You're bleeding."

"It's from the glass." Seemingly disinterested

in his injury, Johnny called 9-1-1, and then tucked his phone away. "An officer should be here soon."

She shrank back at the sight of a blossoming bloodstain on his gray zip-up hoodie. "How do you know you weren't shot?"

Johnny shook his head. "Did you hear the shot? It wasn't that loud. I'll bet we'll discover it was a BB gun and nothing more. It was the glass that cut me, not a small BB."

"Oh." She blinked away his comment, trying to process what had just happened.

He refocused his eyes on her and ran his fingers gently across her hair. "Are you okay?" He plucked a shard of glass out of her hair and held it up for inspection before tossing it aside.

Her leg started shaking and she could feel the chill work its way up her spine. "I think I'm okay." She glanced down at her hands, figuring if she could steady her hands, she'd be all right.

Her hands kept shaking and half her mouth tipped into a smile. "I guess I'm as okay as anyone who just had the glass shot out of her front door would be."

The intensity of Johnny's gaze as he studied her made her feel both protected and afraid. He traced the lines of her cheekbones, inspecting her face. She closed her eyes briefly and tried to tamp down her growing feelings.

He's just protecting you. Nothing more. It's his job.

"I don't think you have any cuts. Does anything hurt?"

She shook her head.

Only then did he turn his attention to his arm. He yanked off his hoodie, undid his shoulder harness and set it and the gun on the counter next to the sink. He pulled his shirt over his head and stood there in a white T-shirt, its sleeve tinged with deep red.

She suddenly felt woozy, so she looked away. She couldn't exactly pass out from the sight of blood when he was the one who had been hurt.

He grabbed a wad of paper towel from the roll next to the sink and, if she had been brave enough to look, she might have seen him pull a piece of glass from his arm. She shuddered at the thought. When she did look up, he was pressing a paper towel to his wound and adhering it with silver duct tape.

"Um, you might regret that."

"The tape?" He shook his head. "I know what I'm doing."

Ellie stood. "Here, sit."

Johnny waved her off and she sat back down. "Did you get a good look at the guy?" He had slipped back into FBI mode.

"Motorcycle. Helmet." She shrugged, rewinding the memory in her mind. "Wheels screeching. I wouldn't be able to tell you more than that. It was dark. I'm not even sure of the color of the bike or helmet."

Johnny rubbed his jaw and nodded.

Ellie pulled her arms close to her and threaded her fingers together in her lap, primarily to keep them from shaking. She finally got the nerve to ask the question she feared the most. "Am I going to have to close the shop to be safe?"

"It might be the smartest thing to do."

He looked down at her and they locked gazes. She felt a connection and just as quickly it was gone. Ellie stood and touched his good arm. Duke circled them, whimpered forlornly and settled at Johnny's feet.

"This store is everything to me."

A loud banging on the interior door leading to the shop made Ellie jump. "Agent Rock? You in there?"

Bang. Bang. Bang. The door rattled in its frame.

Duke jumped to his feet and barked at the intruder. Johnny patted the dog's head. "Easy, boy."

Johnny grabbed his gun off the counter. He held up his finger to silence her as he moved toward the door. He unlocked it and eased forward, his gun at the ready.

"Whoa, it's Officer Bailey. Easy there, Agent." Ellie heard the slightly annoyed, booming voice of the police officer, but he hadn't yet come into view. Johnny opened the door all the way.

Officer Bailey stepped inside and looked from Ellie to Johnny and back.

"Seems to be a lot of excitement for a little shop." He hooked his thumb through his belt and rolled up on the balls of his feet. "Maybe it's time you told us everything you know, Miss Winters."

Ellie's face grew white at Officer Bailey's insinuation. She lifted a shaky hand and pointed a finger at him. "I'll tell you what I know." Her voice was deceptively hard-edged. "I know someone shot out my front door with a BB gun. Someone attacked me in my storage room. And someone threw a brick at my back door. Tell me what you know, Officer Bailey."

Ignoring her last comment, Bailey turned to Johnny. "You think it was a BB gun?"

"Based on the sound, yeah." Johnny glanced at Ellie whose chest was heaving. From the dark look in her eyes, he'd bet it was more from anger at being dismissed than from fear over what had just happened.

"Let's take a look." Johnny thought it best to get Officer Bailey away from Ellie. It was apparent there was tension between the two. Perhaps because Officer Bailey resented her brother for being arrested and inadvertently dismantling the high school baseball team he'd been a part of on their way to the state championship.

Some things a man couldn't forgive. If a guy cut in on his girl or if someone stole their high school state championship, denying them a lifetime of bragging rights.

Johnny looped Duke's leash around the chair and patted his head. "Stay here. I'll be right back." He didn't want the dog to get any glass in his paws. Duke lay down and rested his head on his paws. Poor animal was exhausted from all the excitement.

Their shoes crunched on the broken glass as they made their way to the front of the store. Ellie hung back, wrapping her arms around her middle, cupping her elbows. He wished he could offer her more comfort right now, but he knew his efforts would be rebuked, especially in front of Officer Bailey.

A small breeze picked up and knocked over a picture frame. It landed with a thwack on the glass shelf. Johnny righted it. "Who do you guys use for emergency closures?"

Mickey Bailey rubbed his chin. "Give Curtis at the hardware store a call." The officer dug into his wallet and pulled out a bent business card. "Here, call his cell. He'll come down here last-minute, at a price mind you, and close this place up." He cut a glance to the door. "Supposed to rain later."

Johnny held up a finger and made the call. When he was done, he said to Ellie, "Once Curtis gets here, I'll take you home."

Ellie nodded but didn't say anything. She had gotten a little more color in her cheeks since he had thrown her to the ground in an effort to protect her. If he had been the praying type, he would have thanked God for keeping her safe.

A younger officer, probably a new recruit, stood off to the side and took lots of notes, stopping only to push his hat back on his head. His pure eagerness made Johnny imagine the young officer probably had never responded to a drive-by shooting.

Johnny pointed to a small BB lodged in the wall.

Officer Bailey cut Johnny a sideways glance. "What do you make of this? Were they gunning for you or Ellie?"

Johnny rubbed his jaw and winced, then glanced down at the wadded-up paper towel and duct tape he had stuffed under the sleeve of his T-shirt to soak up the blood. "It has to tie in to the other harassment of late."

Bailey glanced over at Ellie, who seemed distracted. He leaned in. "Does she know why you're in town?"

Johnny nodded.

"You think this one's hands are clean? You know her brother claimed the same thing."

Anger roiled in Johnny's gut. But the officer was right to be suspicious. Things weren't always as they seemed. "I believe she's caught in the middle here. I'm going to stay close to make sure she's safe."

"Staying close serves more than one purpose." Bailey quirked an eyebrow. "In case your gut is wrong."

Johnny bit back a comment. Now was not the time to let his personal feelings get in the way.

Mickey Bailey gestured to Johnny's arm wound with his chin. "You gonna get that checked out?"

"It's fine."

"Might get infected."

"You worry about finding this guy." Johnny pointed at the blown-out door. "I'll worry about me."

Bailey seemed to be contemplating something for a minute. "You wouldn't be the first guy to be distracted by a pretty face."

Johnny shook his head. "I'm going to pretend you didn't say that."

"Say what?" The two men turned around and found Ellie standing a foot away from them, a look of worry pinching her features. Ellie Winters was certainly a pretty face.

"Agent Rock is giving me his theory on what happened here."

Ellie crossed her arms. "Oh?"

"Nothing more than you already know," Johnny said.

Officer Bailey shifted his stance, as if he had suddenly remembered something. "Hey, didn't you have some kids from the church helping around here? What were their names?"

Ellie dropped her arms to her side. "Yes, Collin Parker and Kerry Pitz." She dragged her fingers through her hair. "Why do you ask?"

Mickey Bailey frowned. "I'm sorry to tell you this, but an ambulance just rushed Kerry to the hospital."

Ellie leaned heavily on the counter, looking as though her knees were about to give out on her. "Was that the ambulance I heard?"

"Must have been." Bailey stuffed his hand into his pants' pocket and jiggled his change. "His mom found him unresponsive in his bedroom."

Johnny wrapped an arm around Ellie's waist; a part of him expected her to push him away. "What happened?"

"Drugs. One of my officers, who lives in the neighborhood, was first to arrive. He saw a discarded syringe on the scene."

Ellie leaned into Johnny, her thin frame tucking neatly into his side. "Oh, no." Her voice sounded small.

"I realize this might not be the time to mention it, but any chance any of the young men you hired to work here might have used your address to ship drugs?" Johnny asked.

Officer Bailey did that obnoxious thing with his change again. *Ching-ching-ching.*

"They're good boys. I've known them for years. I volunteered as a mother's helper in their preschool class at Sunday school when I was a young girl. And I volunteered in their summer vacation Bible school when I was in high school. I still serve as a chaperone at outings."

"Seems Kerry, at least, has gone off the rails," the officer said.

"Is he going to be okay?" Johnny asked, watching the officer for any clues that he might be soft selling on account of Ellie.

"The officer said they're working on him." Bailey exhaled loudly. "Where there's life, there's hope."

Ellie stood straighter and stepped away from Johnny. He immediately missed her warmth, their connection. She closed her eyes briefly and then opened them. "This is a nightmare." Her trusting gaze lingered on his. "You have to find whoever's doing this before any more kids die."

"I will." And that was a promise Johnny intended to keep.

Johnny climbed out of the back of the police cruiser with Ellie when they reached her house. She spun around and said, "I'm fine," in response to the look of concern on Johnny's face.

Johnny subtly shook his head as Duke sniffed the ground by his feet. "I want to see you in. Make sure you're safe."

Johnny patted the hood of the police car and leaned in toward the open window. "Can you swing back in thirty minutes and pick me up?" he asked the officer.

"Sure thing."

Ellie watched the patrol car drive off until the red taillights disappeared at the turn.

She turned toward her garage apartment. "I had hoped for an exciting opening week at the shop, but this is a little ridiculous." She had envisioned smiling customers, lines at the register and ordering new merchandise. Attacks in the storeroom, shots through the window and Curtis from the hardware store nailing plywood to the door had not entered her brain. Even in her wildest imagination.

Johnny scratched his forehead. "Curtis has the

shop sealed up for now. Get a good night's sleep then decide what you want to do in the morning."

Ellie's dull headache had blossomed into a *thud-thud-thud* that would surely keep her up. She groaned.

"You okay?"

She laughed; a mirthless sound. "If the incidents at the shop weren't bad enough, now Kerry…" She shook her head. *Please, Lord, let Kerry be okay.* "His poor parents. He has a little brother, too. I can't imagine what they're going through."

"I don't know him. But…" He let the words dangle out there, as if he wanted to say more but something was stopping him. "Let's get inside. You don't mind Duke?"

"Of course not." Ellie leaned over and patted the dog's head. As they climbed the stairs to her apartment, she glanced over toward her mother's house. The flickering of the TV screen was visible through the family room window. Her mother was probably dozing on the couch.

Ellie unlocked the door and stepped into the small space. She felt for the light switch on the wall and flipped it, casting the room in a warm glow. The place wasn't much, but it was hers. *All hers.* She had lived alone in Buffalo, but her boyfriend had been a constant critic of her choices in furniture, paint colors and TV shows.

She couldn't do anything without his comments. All negative.

It was a wonder she'd stayed with him so long, but it's amazing—and sad—what someone will do when they think they have no choice. She had mistakenly thought her boyfriend was her ticket out of this Podunk-like town and to independence, but he had trapped her in an even crueler prison. It was only after she realized he was cheating on her that his pleas of "don't leave me" and "you'll never find anyone else" fell on deaf ears. If her choice in life was him or no one else, she'd gladly settle for the latter.

"Nice place," Johnny said, shifting his stance in the doorway.

"It'll do. For now." Ellie turned to face Johnny and a warm rush surrounded her heart. Johnny was someone. Inwardly she smiled. Her range of emotions was all over the place. She was in no position to be thinking romantic thoughts toward anyone, especially Johnny Rock, the law-enforcement agent responsible for her brother's wrongful arrest.

The man investigating a shipment of drugs to her store.

Ellie rolled her shoulders, trying to ease the knots. "Stay for tea?" She hoped her tone didn't sound desperate.

"Sounds good." He closed the door behind

them and Ellie thought about her mother next door. What would she say about her entertaining a man in her apartment? She quickly shook away the thought. They were only having tea.

Besides, they had Duke for a chaperone. She smiled inwardly at the silly thought.

Ellie opened the cabinet on the far wall, a space that had been converted into a small kitchen. She pulled out two mugs and two tea bags. She glanced over her shoulder and noticed Johnny wince as he tugged off his hoodie.

"You should probably get that cut checked out," Ellie said, coming around to his side of the island.

His mouth twisted as he shook his head. "Nah."

Ellie held up a finger and crossed to the bathroom. She didn't exactly have a medical kit, she wasn't even sure she had a Band-Aid, but she did find cotton balls, alcohol and a princess Band-Aid left over from when her niece had visited.

She gathered up the supplies and marched back into the kitchen.

"I'm no Florence Nightingale, but we need to clean your arm." She lifted her eyes to meet his.

Something unspoken stretched between them. Johnny searched her eyes. It appeared he wanted to say something when he suddenly glanced down at the princess bandage on the counter and broke the spell. "Is that all you have?" He gave her the cutest lopsided smile. "I think princesses might cut into my toughness factor."

"There's no danger there." She laughed nervously at the boldness of her comment. Face firing hot, she focused all her attention on his arm. His muscled arm.

No, no, no.

She blinked a few times. His injury. Focus on that.

She picked at the edge of the duct tape stuck to his flesh. Ellie got hold of a corner between her index finger and thumb. "This might sting a bit."

His eyebrow arched as if to say, "You think?"

"I remember someone telling me he knew what he was doing." She mimicked his expression.

"Just do it already."

"One, two, three—" She yanked at the duct tape and Johnny let out a laugh-groan.

"Oh, man, a princess Band-Aid is looking better by the minute."

Ellie laughed. "Sorry." She peeled back the paper towel sticking to his wound. It was her turn to wince. "This might need stitches."

Johnny inspected the wound. "It's fine." She had a feeling he was going to say *fine* no matter how it looked.

"Well," Ellie said hesitantly, "let me wash it out."

"Hurry up and just do it, then." Johnny flexed

his muscle and glanced away as if bracing himself.

Holding the alcohol and cotton swab, she pulled her head back and studied him. "You're afraid of a little rubbing alcohol?"

He cut her an annoyed sideways glance. "Do it already."

Ellie rubbed the cotton swab as gently as she could over the wound. Johnny flinched.

"Almost done," she said reassuringly, just as she would do if she were cleaning a skinned knee on her niece.

Ellie tore the wrapper off the Band-Aid and picked off the tabs from the adhesive. She lined up the princess bandage with his wound and pressed it to his skin. "There, there," she said with humor in her voice as she smoothed her hand over the Band-Aid.

Johnny traced the creased edge of the bandage and a smile tilted the corners of his mouth. "Thanks."

Ellie spun around, needing to create some distance. "No problem. Still want that tea?"

"What? No lollipop?"

"Ha, ha." She filled the kettle, set it on the stove and turned the dial to high. Deep inside her purse, she could hear her phone ringing. She plucked it out and saw her brother's name on the caller ID.

"Hey," she said when she answered.

"You okay? Roger called to say there had been some sort of shooting at your store. He said he was closing up his sub shop and saw the commotion. I wasn't sure if he was pulling my leg." Greg's voice held a hint of humor, as if he feared he had been the subject of a prank and didn't want to fall for it.

"I'm fine. And, yes, it's true. Some kid with a BB gun."

"Johnny was with you?"

"Yeah."

Her brother made a sound she couldn't quite distinguish. If Johnny hadn't been standing right across the island from her, she would have told her brother to mind his own business, that, yes, she remembered what Johnny's false accusations had done to their family, but she had her own reason for hanging out with him.

Something in her heart shifted at the sight of Johnny's muscled bicep with the sweet little princess Band-Aid.

He was her protector. Yes, her protector. Nothing more.

She turned her back to Johnny and leaned on the counter, crossing her one free arm over her middle. "I have to go."

"You probably should run over and tell Mom

before she hears it from one of her friends. She'll be worried."

"Yes, Greg…" She dragged out the words. He was right, but she hated to be told what to do.

"One more thing. Sorry it's late notice, but it looks like it's going to be a nice day tomorrow. Beth and I thought we'd have a few friends and family over for a last cookout of the season. Might be snowing soon, never know around here. Why don't you come over?"

"What time?"

"How about after you close the shop? You close around five on Saturday, right?"

"Yes." She wasn't sure *if* or how long she'd be open tomorrow considering what had happened tonight, but she didn't feel like getting into that. She forced a cheery tone. "Sounds good. I'll bring a dessert." She'd grab something from the grocery store. At a different time she might have stopped at the bakery next door, but she feared what Mr. Vino might do to something he knew she'd eat.

"I'll tell Beth." He cleared his throat. "Ellie…" A long pause stretched over the line. Her stomach dropped. He'd used the same tone he had when he'd called to say their father had died. Cutting the lawn one minute. Dead inside an ambulance the next.

She shoved the thought away.

"Yeah."

"If there was something going on, you'd tell me, right?"

"Um, yeah." She glanced over her shoulder at Johnny. "There's been some crazy stuff at the shop—"

Ellie heard her niece calling for her father in the background.

"Nothing that can't keep. We'll talk more tomorrow. I'll let you go. Give Grace a hug for me."

Ellie ended the call. She set her cell phone aside and filled the two mugs with hot water.

"You and Greg are close."

Ellie nodded. "More so now as adults. I guess I'm not the annoying little sister anymore." She dunked her tea bag a few times. "But ever since I moved back home, he thinks he's my protector." She shrugged. "Maybe since Dad's gone now."

"You're lucky."

Ellie fingered the charm on her bracelet.

"Family's important. Other than my grandfather, I don't have any family." Johnny tossed his tea bag into the garbage. "My mother died of a drug overdose when I was twelve."

FIVE

"I'm so sorry."

The expression on Ellie's face was a mix of sympathy and disbelief. Johnny was immediately sorry he had shared a bit of his past. Very few people knew about it.

"When my mom died, my grandparents refused to take me in." Johnny pulled out a stool and sat at the island counter. He wasn't sure he'd ever said that out loud to anyone.

"How horrible…"

The compassion in her tone knocked a brick from the wall he had built around his heart. A muscle ticked in his jaw as he struggled to relax his fists, pick up his mug and take a sip of his tea.

Next thing he knew, she was standing next to him, a hand on his back. He stiffened and she pulled her hand away, but her tone didn't change. "Is this why you chose the line of work you're in?"

"Yeah." He struggled to keep his tone even.

"My mom graduated from Williamstown High School." He tapped the countertop with his index finger. "This is where it all started. The beginning of the end."

His eyes drifted to Ellie's, wondering if she'd think differently about him. He didn't know what to feel. Some people knew his story, but not because he'd told them. He had never spoken of his past out loud to anyone other than his grandfather. And then he hadn't really had to; his grandfather had suffered just as much as he had. Or maybe more. His grandfather had had a heavier burden of guilt. As if he somehow hadn't been vigilant enough in protecting his daughter.

Most people didn't realize Johnny felt the burden of guilt, too. Guilt that he hadn't been enough to make his mother stop doing drugs. To get clean.

To stay.

Ellie lifted her eyes to him, but didn't say anything. Johnny bowed his head and rubbed the back of his neck.

"I'm not in this job to mess with people's lives. Well, unless you're a drug dealer." He smiled, hoping to coax the same out of Ellie. The compassion radiating from her warm eyes unnerved him.

"I had heard the rumors after I was an undercover narc at the high school. People might have been biased against me after they learned who my mother was. I had never lived in Williamstown until I arrived as an undercover narcotics officer. That's how I was able to pull it off. But once people learned my real name, who my mother was, they didn't seem very forgiving, especially not after your brother was acquitted. It was as if they shouldn't have expected any more from the son of a druggie."

Ellie tugged at her sleeves and crossed her arms. "This is a difficult conversation. I was thrilled my brother was acquitted. He could have gone to jail for something he hadn't done."

"Well…" Johnny bit back the words, not wanting to go there tonight. "Because your brother went free, people questioned my integrity. People thought I was in it solely to make a name for myself. That I had a huge ego. And that only seemed to bear itself out when I signed on to work for the FBI." His gaze wandered to the artwork adorning the walls. *Ellie's artwork.* He'd recognize her style anywhere.

"My childhood…my upbringing…made me hard. I don't care what people think."

Cocking her head, Ellie made an indecipherable sound and sadness filled her eyes.

Johnny reached out and dared to run a strand of her auburn hair through his fingers. "But for some crazy reason, I care what you think."

Ellie's eyes searched his face. "Why…?"

Johnny wanted to tell her something personal, about how he admired her strength, her quick wit, her fiery temper, but an uneasy feeling in his stomach made him settle on something safer. He had already shared with her the worst part of his childhood.

"Your family was the closest thing to a family I had ever had."

A deep line formed between her eyebrows. "You had my brother arrested. You really must have had a warped perception of family."

"It killed me when your brother got caught up in that mess." It really had. "As a kid, I had been shuffled from one foster home to the next until I turned eighteen. So, yeah, hanging out with your family was pretty cool. I was only twenty-two. I never knew what a stable family looked like."

"What are you saying? I'm like the little sister you never had?"

He thought he detected a trace of disappointment in her voice.

"Something like that." The feelings he found growing for her were far from sisterly. "I used to like talking to you when I stopped over. Your innocence was refreshing. Something I didn't come across often in my own childhood or my line of work."

She tucked in her chin and her cheeks fired a soft pink.

"I remember you always had an easel set up in the kitchen." He held up his palm. "You're very talented."

"Thanks. I had hoped to go to college to study art, but…well…"

"I'm sorry. I really am." But not for the reasons she might have guessed. "I care about you and I want to make sure you're safe while we figure out who's using your address to ship drugs into Williamstown."

Ellie nodded. She looked as though she wanted to say something, but didn't.

Johnny decided to return to safer ground. "You mentioned you knew the kid who overdosed."

"He's part of the youth group at church. We've been meeting on Saturdays to get ready for the fall carnival."

"Are you meeting with the group this weekend? Could we go there and talk to the other youth in the group? Maybe someone knows something."

Ellie pushed the hair away from her face. "We could go tomorrow evening."

"Sounds good."

"I'm going to my brother's for a fall cookout beforehand." She glanced up expectantly. "Why don't you come with me? We can go up to the church afterward."

Johnny must have flinched because Ellie's tone

grew indignant. "You *just* told me you enjoyed hanging out with my family."

"That was before…" He didn't need to finish the sentence.

"Maybe it's time to put this all behind us. They're always preaching about forgiveness at church."

Johnny forced a smile, wondering who she thought needed forgiveness.

"Dinner at your brother's house sounds good." He hoped God wasn't tallying up all his little white lies. A little lie was a small price to pay to keep Ellie safe.

To keep her alive.

"So much for our store, huh?"

The next morning Ashley strolled in past the two local police officers who were wrapping up their investigation of the drive-by shooting while Ellie swept up the glass.

Anger and annoyance mixed with the tinkling sound of the shards of glass and the *swoosh-swoosh* of the broom as Ellie quickened her motions.

Ashley had never answered her cell phone until this morning and when she had, she hadn't seemed overly concerned. She'd seemed more annoyed that now a trip to the shop would cut into her weekend plans.

Ellie should have never gone into business with anyone. She had wanted to be independent. But lack of financing had trumped that.

Ellie tracked Ashley's movements as she tip-toed around the glass.

"I could use some help cleaning up." Ellie bit the words out.

Ashley's pinched expression told Ellie what she thought of that. "That's why we have insurance." She glanced down at her fingernails as if thinking better of ruining her manicure.

Ellie stopped and rested her elbow on the broom. "We have insurance to cover the big stuff. I don't think they're going to come in here and clean up the glass."

Ashley turned up her nose and flattened her hand over her expensive-looking sweater. "I didn't come dressed for hard labor." She let out a long sigh. "What exactly happened here?" Her tone seemed more appropriate for when a pet soiled on the carpet, not a life-and-death situation.

Ellie thought about the terror pumping through her veins as the shots had rung out. "Johnny wants to talk to both of us this morning." They had to let Ashley know about the ongoing drug investigation. It was obvious someone was trying to intimidate them and her poor friend had no idea what was really going on.

Johnny appeared in the doorway, holding a tray of coffee. "Did I hear my name?"

"Yes." Ellie leaned the broom up against the wall. "Ashley wants to know what's going on."

Johnny gave Ellie a brief nod and set the coffee on the counter. "I wasn't sure how you liked it, so I got a couple black coffees with cream and sugar packets on the side."

"Thanks." Ellie grabbed a coffee, tore off the lid, poured two sugars and two creams into the black liquid, and stirred. Ashley stood there with her arms crossed, obviously preferring her lattes to a good old cup of joe.

The sound of glass crunching drew their attention to the doorway. Tony stood there with a shocked expression on his face. "What happened here? Everyone okay?" The young man seemed paler than usual, probably due to knowing the shop only feet from his father's bakery had been vandalized.

Ashley stepped forward before Ellie had a chance to speak. "Someone shot out the glass on the door." She nearly petted the sleeve of Tony's white coat. "I was so lucky I didn't work last night. But it could have been me."

Tony's eyes drifted to Ellie. "Did you see who did this?"

She shook her head, unable to find the words

to explain once again how the helmeted shooter had zipped by too fast on a motorcycle. When her vague response obviously didn't suit him, he asked, "Were you alone?"

"I was with her," Johnny said.

Tony's eyebrows rose and something flitted across his face that she couldn't quite read.

Tony stepped away from Ashley, a hint of annoyance flashing on his face. "My father and I are worried about the few incidences here. Our shop is *right* next door. Do you think these are isolated events? Should we be concerned?"

"Concern would be an appropriate response," Johnny said matter-of-factly. "We have reason to believe someone is targeting this gift shop because of a drug shipment."

"Drugs, really?" Tony asked, running a hand across his mussed hair. "That's messed up."

Ellie turned to Ashley. "Any chance you found a strange package and stashed it somewhere? Something you might have forgotten about?"

Ashley scratched her head, as if it helped her to think. "I thought those monkey things you ordered were weird." She did her usual deflecting with humor.

Ellie huffed her frustration. "No, nothing like that. Anything that looked suspicious? Drugs?"

"No," Ashley said, disbelief and annoyance

lacing her tone. "Don't you think I would have told you if I had?"

Ellie hoped so.

"Listen—" Ashley waved around her hand "—I went into business with you because I thought it would be fun."

Ellie's heart began to race as she waited for Ashley to admit going into the gift shop business had been a mistake.

Ashley flicked a strand of hair over her shoulder. "This shop has become a real drag. And…" She let the word hang there for emphasis, the way she usually did when she was waiting for all eyes to turn to her. "I'm not an ATM machine. I can't afford to keep throwing money into a lame business venture."

And there it was.

"It takes time to grow a business." Ellie swallowed hard, trying to keep the desperation out of her voice, something she'd rarely achieved when she'd pleaded with her former boyfriend. Ellie hated that side of her—the weak, supplicant girl.

"I understand, but we're going to have to adjust things." Ashley crossed her arms. "Mainly, I don't plan on working here." She jerked her thumb toward the plywood propped up near the door. "I'm not up for getting shot at."

"Who is?" Ellie said, her pulse whooshing in her ears. "You can't bail on me now."

"This isn't productive," Johnny interrupted. "We need to clean up the shop and take precautions."

Tony frowned. "I thought you were in town to help your grandfather move. Are the rumors true? Are you saying you're investigating drugs running through Williamstown?"

"Yes." Johnny studied Tony carefully over his coffee cup. "Do you have any information you'd like to share?"

Tony's eyes flared wide. "No. Not at all. I'm concerned because my family's business is next door."

Johnny nodded. "Have you noticed any unusual people hanging around outside? In the alley? You work long hours at the bakery, right?"

"Yeah, sure." Tony rubbed his jaw, as if he was giving it some thought. "Can't say I've seen anything unusual, but I'll be sure to keep my eyes open."

Johnny looked as though he wanted to say something but suddenly his stern expression softened. "Can't hurt to have more eyes." He reached into his pocket and handed Tony his card. "Call me if you see anything." He paused a fraction. "Or if you remember anything."

Tony brushed a kiss on Ashley's cheek. "I have to get back to work." Ashley muttered something Ellie couldn't hear.

Her business partner spun around. "Should I be afraid?" She batted her eyelashes at Johnny, not looking one bit afraid. "Working at the store to sell a few birthday cards isn't worth the hassle."

"You can't..." Ellie swallowed hard. She wanted to wipe the sympathetic look off Johnny's face. She didn't want or need his sympathy.

"I think you need to shut down the store. Until we catch this guy." Johnny reached out to touch her hand, but Ellie pulled away.

"Wait—what?"

"It's not safe. You've had two near misses in a matter of days. Someone obviously has it out for you."

"Yes, I agree. We should close the store." Ashley tucked a strand of light blond hair behind her ear.

"Wait a minute. Ashley, we can't just close the doors. It will drive us out of business. I've already explained all this."

Her friend shrugged, as if losing Gifts and More would be no big deal. Ellie's heart sank. Of course it would be no big deal for her friend. She could take her money and do something else. Whereas, this shop was all Ellie had. It was far more than simply a job to her.

The concern in Johnny's eyes made her pause. Nausea welled in Ellie's gut. Her dream was crumbling around her and someone wanted to hurt her.

Or worse.

Drinking coffee wasn't exactly the best way to calm his frazzled nerves. Johnny set his cup on a shelf in the gift shop and grabbed the broom from its resting spot against the wall.

Ellie shook her head. "I got it." She took the broom from him rather abruptly, their fingers brushing in the exchange.

"How well do you know Tony?" Johnny asked Ashley, who didn't seem to be in much of a hurry to leave for someone who had just announced she wasn't going to work at the shop anymore, or at least until the perpetrator was caught.

Something about the baker had struck a nerve with Johnny. Had the young baker been solely concerned with the safety of his own shop? The well-being of the quiet community? Or was there something else going on there?

Ashley scrunched her nose. "I know him as well as anyone I've only dated a few weeks. I mean, I've known him since high school—this is a small town—but we've only been dating for a few weeks." Then came her bland compliment. "He's nice enough. A little stressed about work, but who isn't? Tough economy, right?"

"Yeah." Though Johnny hadn't said anything

to Ellie yet, he'd had the FBI run a check on Tony. The bakery was in some serious debt. Not unheard of with business owners, but enough to make Tony take up dealing drugs as a side business? He'd have to talk to the man later without an audience. Tony Vino was obviously shaken up and maybe his nerves would make him crack.

If he had something to crack about.

Ashley smiled demurely, as if having second thoughts. "I'll go home and change and come back to help clean up."

Johnny held up his hand. "I'll stay and help Ellie."

Ellie looked as if she was about to protest, but she didn't say a word.

"Well, okay." Ashley stepped daintily around the broken glass. "I'm gonna scoot, then."

Johnny wondered why Ashley had even invested her money in the shop when she obviously didn't care about it. Were she and Ellie such good friends that she just wanted to help her friend out financially? Something niggled at the base of his brain. Her ties with Tony also bothered him. He made a mental note as they watched Ashley leave.

Ellie turned to Johnny. "You realize this will be the end of my shop. The dream will die before it even gets off the ground." She paused a second, as if afraid to reveal the tremble in her voice.

"It's not over. My priority is to make sure

you're safe." He glanced over at the two officers chatting by the register. "If you guys are done, you can file your report at Williamstown PD headquarters. Ellie Winters and I will wrap things up here."

Coffee cups in hand, the two officers left. Two gentlemen from the hardware store were installing a new door.

Ellie placed the broom against the wall and sat slowly on the stool behind the register, the look in her eyes reminiscent of one he had seen a million years ago. Leaning on the counter, she planted her chin in the palm of her hand. "I don't know why I bothered."

"With the shop?"

"Yeah. I knew it was a long shot to begin with. I had no idea I'd be asked to close down due to a drive-by shooting the first week I was open." Her tone indicated she wasn't convinced she'd actually close the shop.

Johnny leaned a hip on the counter, his thigh brushing against Ellie's knee. "I'm sorry, Ellie. I'll do whatever I can to get your shop back open." He scanned the space. The back half of the store was untouched as a result of last night's events. So were several unopened boxes in the back room. "Do you have boxes stored anywhere else but here?"

Ellie sat upright and bit her bottom lip. "I have

some in my parents' basement, but nothing that was originally shipped to this address. Those boxes are pieces I've collected over the years. Antiques, photo frames, trinkets. Stuff I haven't had time, or room, to display."

Johnny patted the counter next to him. "Okay, I don't think that's what we're looking for."

Ellie wrapped her arms around her middle. "You say you believe me when I tell you I have nothing to do with this."

Johnny's stomach bottomed out. He did believe her. But he doubted she'd be happy if she found out he had run checks on her brother and Roger since they had been previously arrested for dealing drugs. Both seemed to have kept their noses clean. Experience told him that those reports didn't always reveal the big picture.

"What happens if you find something on my property? What does that make me…guilty of possession of drugs?" She shook her head in disbelief. "Should I call a lawyer? Just to be safe?"

All the color drained from her face as if she was mentally reliving her family's experience when her brother had been arrested.

He reached out and stopped her hand midway to shoving her hair out of her eyes again. "You have to do what's best for you." That was the logical advice. His professional advice. "But I'd hate for you to have to spend the money on legal fees. I know it's tight with the shop."

Ellie's lower lip quivered, as if she were on the verge of crying.

"I know you're not involved and I'm doing everything I can to find out who is. Can you trust me on this?"

She lifted her eyes to him with an unspoken "Why?"

"More than once I saw the look in your eyes after the arrest and trial of your brother. That experience devastated you. You'd never do that to your family. Not on purpose."

"You seem quite sure of yourself."

"Am I wrong?"

She shook her head slowly. "But look at my brother. He got wrapped up in something that wasn't even his fault."

Johnny studied the gray slate floor tiles. Her brother Greg had always been the Golden Boy. Still was. Could Johnny ever convince her otherwise? What point would it serve, especially when she was already so hurt? Johnny didn't want to be responsible for putting any more hurt in that sweet woman's eyes.

SIX

"Go on ahead."

Later that afternoon Johnny gestured with his free hand to Ellie to walk ahead of him. Greg Winters's front walkway and porch were adorned with hay bales and pumpkins, all ready for fall.

Ellie smiled and brushed past him, her hands occupied with a white casserole dish. He wondered when she'd had time to bake considering how busy they had been cleaning up the shop.

Johnny stepped up next to Ellie on the small stoop. "Does your mother know about the incident at the gift shop?"

"Yes," Ellie hissed abruptly as she glanced at the door. "I promised her I'd be careful. And just so you know, I am not convinced I'm going to close the shop."

"Can we discuss it further?"

"Perhaps we can discuss ways to keep me safe while I'm working."

"Good point." Ellie was one stubborn woman.

"Maybe I'll win points with your mother for protecting you?" He couldn't help but smile.

Ellie laughed; a genuine laugh that warmed his heart. "I fear she might have wished *you* had been shot." She tipped her head and her hair fell in a mask, hiding her face, as if she couldn't believe she had just said that. "I'm just kidding. She's a good Christian woman."

"Who happens to hold a grudge against me."

Ellie laughed again, as if she didn't truly know what her mother would do when it came down to getting him out of their lives. "All things considered, I can't say I blame her."

"Do you?"

"Do I...?" Ellie angled her head.

Johnny suspected she knew full well what he was talking about, but she was stalling. "Do you still blame me for ruining your brother's life?"

Ellie glanced at the screen door. "You picked a fine time to bring this up." She shook her head curtly, as if to dismiss his question, and leaned on the doorbell with her elbow. A soft chime sounded inside the house followed by running feet.

A little girl with long brown hair in two braids answered, smiling up at them. "Aunt Ellie."

The little girl pushed open the door and Ellie shouldered it to keep it from closing. She kissed the crown of her niece's head. Ellie gestured to

Johnny with her chin. "Grace, this is my friend Mr. Rock."

"Hello," the little girl said, tipping her head to look up at him.

"Nice to meet you, Grace."

"Is everyone in the backyard?" Ellie asked as she walked through the small family room littered with dolls toward a neat kitchen in the back of the house.

"Yes! We're having a party!" Grace ran ahead and opened the sliding screen to the back porch. Ellie set the casserole dish on the stove and Johnny put the refreshments he had purchased on the counter.

Laughter floated in from outside. Johnny silently communicated a quick, "Here goes nothing," before she stepped out onto the back patio.

He followed, not fully understanding why his nerves were wound tighter than when he'd squared off with a gun-toting criminal in a dark alley.

Apparently sensing his unease, Ellie tossed a smile at him. "They don't bite."

His eyes flared wide in feigned distress.

"Come on."

About fifteen adults and a smattering of children were hanging out in the yard. Some were seated around tables, others were playing a game that involved slamming a Frisbee into a black barrel.

"Ah, you made it." A pretty woman, a little older than Ellie, was the first to greet them. Holding a glass of lemonade in one hand, she hugged Ellie with the other and then turned to Johnny. "Hi. I'm Beth Winters, Greg's wife."

"Johnny Rock. I'm—"

Ellie jumped in before he could say anything. "A friend of mine."

"Well, nice to meet you. Grab a drink and some refreshments. We're very casual around here." She smiled and lifted her glass. "We're happy Ellie could bring a friend." Beth smiled warmly at her sister-in-law.

Ellie blushed.

Apparently, Ellie didn't bring male friends around. For some reason, the idea pleased him.

"We're blessed to have perfect weather for one last outdoor party. So make yourself comfortable." Beth's eyes flared wide and she scooted off after a small boy wandering dangerously close to a bigger child determined to test the laws of physics on the swing.

The invisible but very real feeling of awkwardness pushed down on him. Half the people here—the half who didn't know him—would assume he was Ellie's boyfriend. The other half—the half that knew the truth—were shooting him die-man-die daggers with their eyes.

Speaking of which, Ellie's mother called to her

from her lawn chair under the shade of a wide umbrella. "I see you brought a date?" Her voice hitched up on the last word.

"Johnny was helping me clean up at the store," he heard Ellie say as he stepped up beside her. "I thought it polite to invite him for dinner."

Nancy Winters's gaze swept over him, as if she couldn't decide whether to keep up the fight or let it go. She ran her hand along the sun-faded faux wood on the arm of the outdoor chair. "Thank you for keeping my Ellie safe." She shook her head. "Can't believe the crazy goings-on in this world."

Mrs. Winters pushed to a standing position and lurched forward, touching his arm when she lost her footing on an uneven paver. She lowered her voice. "I really do appreciate it, but please don't cause any more trouble for our family."

"No, ma'am." Johnny shook his head for emphasis.

"Mom," Greg said in a voice that seemed louder than necessary, "isn't it great to see Johnny again?" The smile on Greg's sun-tanned and freckled face seemed strained. "I think we can let bygones be bygones. Enjoy a nice meal together." Johnny figured Greg's cordial greeting was strictly for his mother's benefit.

Nancy Winters lifted a shoulder then lowered herself into the chair again. Johnny lunged forward and steadied the arm, the old fold-up chair nearly collapsing with Mrs. Winters inside.

Next to him, Ellie laughed. "Careful, Mom."

Her mother waved her hand in dismissal, but her cheeks flared red.

Maybe I've scored a few points for saving her from the embarrassing fate of ending up head over heels in the folded lawn chair.

Greg smiled at Johnny, a smile that didn't reach his eyes. "It's been a long time."

"Yes, it has." The conversation seemed strained. "Nice home. Beautiful family. You've done well for yourself."

"Thank you. It wasn't without a few bumps along the way." Had Johnny detected an accusation in Greg's tone?

"I had a job to do."

Greg smiled at an older woman who brushed past, then turned his attention back to Johnny. "I had thought we were friends back in high school. I was surprised how well you played us all." His neutral affect was hard to read.

Johnny thought back to the days when Greg had met him in senior homeroom and invited him to the house for dinner. Johnny had never been around a normal house where everyone sat together for dinner. Sometimes he'd miss dinner altogether because his mother had spent her entire paycheck on drugs and cigarettes.

Johnny looked down and saw Ellie was staring up at him. He had obviously missed whatever she had been saying. "I'm sorry, what?"

"What would you like to drink?"

"I'm good for now."

"I wanted to tell you," Greg said, "Roger Petersen and his wife are coming over."

Johnny ran a hand through his hair.

"Roger has turned his life around since getting out of prison. He doesn't live far from here."

Johnny already knew that. He had run checks on all the players from ten years ago.

"So be nice." Greg smiled stiffly. "I didn't know you were coming or I would have warned him."

Johnny held his hand up. "I'll play nice." And maybe he could get a read on what these two men had been up to lately. It would crush Ellie if her brother was in any way involved. But it seemed unlikely Greg would put his sister in harm's way.

As if on cue, Roger appeared in the doorway. He pushed open the screen and it hit the edge of the frame with a clack. A dark-haired woman in capris and a pink top came up behind him. "Don't stop in the doorway, Roger."

Roger glared at Johnny. If Johnny hadn't been so focused, he might have missed the subtle quirk of a smile on Roger's face.

What is that all about?

Roger strolled onto the patio and held out his hand. "Johnny Rock. Imagine you here."

"Roger Petersen. In the flesh." Johnny mimicked him, accepting his hand.

Greg stepped between the two men. "I imagine we can all be cordial." He cast a warning toward Roger, then to Johnny.

Roger blinked slowly. "Of course."

Roger's wife came up behind him and rested her chin on her husband's shoulder. Her perfectly straight teeth were visible through her parted lips, tilted into a beaming smile. "Hello."

Roger stepped to the side and wrapped his arm around the slender woman's waist. "This is my wife, Ginger."

Ellie smiled her greeting and nodded in acknowledgment.

Roger squeezed his wife closer to him. "Ginger and I have been house shopping." He lifted his chin and scanned the yard. "We have an appointment to see a house in this very neighborhood. Wouldn't that be great if we became neighbors?"

"Fantastic." Greg smiled but something cool settled in his eyes. "Excuse me for a minute. I have to do some hosting duties."

"Glad things are going well," Johnny said, studying Roger.

Roger smiled coyly. "I've had some tough

breaks, but now I've got a good business. Ever been to the sub shop on Main Street?"

"Can't say I have. I'll have to stop by," Johnny said.

"Do that." The corners of Roger's mouth tugged down as if he were giving something considerable thought. He reached for his wife's hand. "It's nice seeing you, Ellie. Johnny." He nodded. "I think we'll wander over and say hello to Mrs. Winters."

Johnny stepped away from the crowd and whispered to Ellie, "Your brother and Roger hang out a lot?"

Ellie's eyes grew worried. "Greg's a very loyal person. They've been friends since kindergarten. What kind of person would he be if he turned his back on his friend in difficult times?"

Greg wandered over. "Everything okay?"

Ellie's hand went to the hollow of her neck. "Johnny was asking about Roger."

"What about him?" An edge of defensiveness crept into Greg's voice.

"It's okay," Ellie said. "I was trying to explain to Johnny how you've forgiven Roger for getting you caught up in that mess."

Greg slowly blinked. "It's more than that."

A look of confusion swept across Ellie's face.

"We need to talk." Greg glanced over at his wife pushing their daughter on the swing. "Out front."

* * *

"All three of us?" Ellie asked, confusion crowding in on her.

A very somber Greg nodded. She rarely saw this side of her brother. He was always the cliché calm, cool, collected.

The proverbial Golden Boy.

Ellie's heart raced, just as it had when she'd seen her mother's face after her father died. Ellie referred to those moments as defining. In one moment, life changed. How you handled it defined you.

"Are you going to get the hot dogs on the grill?" an alarmed Beth called out from the far corner of the yard where she seemed stuck supervising the kids climbing all over the wooden play set. The play set her brother had taken three solid weekends to build from a blueprint purchased online. He really was a good dad.

"Be right back, honey." Greg plastered on a smile and waved. "I promise."

Her brother led them around the side of the house and toward the minivan parked in the driveway, perhaps where he felt he was far enough from his guests. He leaned against the side of the maroon vehicle and studied his feet.

"What is it? Is everything okay?" Ellie's nerve endings buzzed. Was someone sick? Had something happened?

Johnny momentarily placed his hand on Ellie's arm.

Greg took a deep breath and released it. His eyes flicked up over Ellie's head, undoubtedly to meet Johnny's gaze.

The vulnerable look on her brother's face was a strange juxtaposition to the sunny fall day and the yellow mums planted around the tree near the street. The perfect fall afternoon.

"I wasn't as innocent as you think." Greg spit out the words in a burst of confidence that belied his trembling hands.

Ellie's stomach bottomed out. "What are you talking about?"

Greg closed his eyes for a long minute then opened them again. "I *was* guilty of dealing drugs in high school."

Ellie gasped and leaned back, bumping into Johnny. Nausea clawed at her throat but spewing her guts on the driveway wasn't high on her list right now. Johnny's solid hands steadied her at the waist. She swallowed hard and focused all her energy on staying calm. As she had when she'd approached her boyfriend about the inappropriate photos on his cell phone.

"What?"

"I stupidly got involved with selling drugs." His shoulders slouched. "The only reason I got off was because Dad and Mom got the best lawyer."

The world seemed to close in around Ellie. The birds chirping got more distant. The blades of grass grew more defined. She blinked away her disorientation. She sensed, rather than heard, Johnny saying something to her. She couldn't make out the words. She raised her hand, needing silence.

"Does Mom know?" Tiny stars danced in her eyes. She feared a migraine coming on. A niggle of doubt slithered into her brain. Their mother had been their brother's staunchest supporter. She hadn't been putting on an act, too. Had she?

No, no, no…

Her mother couldn't have known.

Greg shook his head. "Dad never knew, either."

Ellie pressed her hand to her heart. At least part of her world hadn't tilted off its axis.

Greg shifted his feet. "I was so ashamed." His voice grew very quiet. "Still am."

"How could you have done that?" She hated the squeaky quality of her voice. "How?"

"Stupid, I guess." She had never heard her brother sound so weak. So small. *Poof!* Gone was the image of her older brother, the one she had forever looked up to.

"Mom and Dad had given me every opportunity and I had let them down. I couldn't face them if they had known I had done it. I was a coward."

"Why?" A throbbing pounded behind her eyes. "Did Roger put you up to it?"

"I made my own bad decisions. It was so easy at first. Easy money, you know? Next thing I knew, the police were pounding on the door and I'm getting arrested."

Ellie shoved a hand through her hair. "Why are you telling me now?"

"I've heard the news about the second drug overdose."

Ellie's mouth grew dry. "What does that have to do with what happened ten years ago?" Her eyes grew wide. "Oh, no, you're not…" She struggled to fill her heavy lungs with air. The image of his wife Beth herding the children in the backyard flooded her mind. He'd destroy them. "No…"

"Oh, no, no. Absolutely not. I would never… I mean…" Greg stumbled over his words. "Not again."

"Why are you speaking up now, Greg?" Johnny's husky voice sounded close to her ear. And then Ellie remembered how she had constantly criticized Johnny for ruining her brother's life. For ruining hers.

Greg had been the architect of his own downfall. He had been the one to cause his parents so much heartache.

Her brother clasped his hands together and closed his eyes briefly. "Beth and I know Kerry from the church. He was a real nice kid who obviously made a bad decision. We need these drugs off the street." He lowered his voice. "Am I right in assuming you're in town investigating?"

"Yes, do you have information?" Johnny glanced toward the yard. Was he also wondering about Roger?

No, Ellie thought. *Roger's married. He's changed.* Didn't God say people could change? Her brother had changed too, right?

"I don't." Greg kicked the tire on the minivan. "I can't believe I was so stupid and it pains me that kids are still killing themselves with this stuff."

"*Stuff* you had willingly sold to *kids*." Hurt lingered with the bile in her gut. Her brother had lied to everyone. Her dreams had been derailed, her parents' retirement gone, all because of her boneheaded brother.

Horror widened Greg's eyes. "I was young. Stupid. I would *never* do anything to jeopardize my family. I'm not that stupid kid anymore."

"Like Johnny said, why tell us now? To ease your stupid conscience?" She spat the words out.

"If I'm being honest? Partially." Greg crossed his arms and leaned back on the minivan. "I told you because I don't want you to doubt Johnny. He's great at what he does." Her big brother's eyes grew dark. Intense. "Trust him to find the bad guys." He gave her the saddest smile that broke her heart. "He did catch the bad guys once." Greg laughed; a thin sound.

Tingles bit at her fingertips.

Greg reached out and touched her arm. "Trust him to keep you safe. He's a good guy."

Ellie curled up her fist and had the most irrational urge to slug her brother in his arm because she couldn't wrap her head around all her emotions. He had put all of them through so much pain. He'd cost his parents a ton in legal fees. He had cost her a college education.

And if you talked to the old men seated on the bench outside the hardware store, their arrest had cost the sleepy town of Williamstown their one chance of earning the state championship in baseball. But Ellie couldn't care one bit about that.

"Beth knows."

Ellie's head shot up. "What?"

"Beth knows. I told her before we got married."

Ellie shook her head, as if it would snap her thoughts into place. "Yet you never told your family." She didn't bother to frame it as a question.

Greg shook his head. His Adam's apple bobbed in his throat. "I owe Johnny my life."

Ellie froze in place and cut a sideways glance to Johnny, who stood expressionless, a muscle ticking in his jaw.

"If Johnny hadn't had me arrested, my life

would have continued down that dark path." Greg shook his head, as if seeing an alternate future. He held out his hand to his well-tended house in the suburbs. "I owe all of this to you. Thank you."

Johnny and Greg shook hands. "I was doing my job," Johnny said. "I had considered you a friend. It tore me up when I realized you were involved with drugs."

"At first I felt betrayed," Greg said. "You were my friend, after all. I thought you were the biggest jerk. A liar. Then, once reality set in, I decided God must have had other plans for me."

Ellie wanted to ask him yet again why he hadn't confessed to his own family, but decided she had already asked twice and both times he'd told her he was ashamed. Only her brother knew his heart.

Well, her brother and God. He'd have to work on his relationship with God and his reasons for not revealing the truth to those he loved.

"Just do me a favor. Don't tell Mom. I'll tell her myself this week."

"Let me know because I'm going to make myself scarce that day." She laughed to release the tension and Greg pulled her into an embrace.

She opened her eyes and found Johnny watching her intently. The feeling unnerved her.

SEVEN

"Thanks for coming out tonight." The pastor, a middle-aged man with a receding hairline and smile lines around his eyes, crossed the gym and shook first Johnny's, then Ellie's hand. They had left the barbecue at her brother's house early in order to talk to the youth group at the church. It was just as well because rain had moved into the area.

"Thanks for letting us talk to the youth. I know they're running short on time to get things ready for the fall carnival next weekend." Ellie tucked her fingers into the back pockets of her jeans and smiled.

The loud *bam-bam-bam* of hammering sounded from the far corner of the gym and the pastor smiled. "These kids are good kids. They'll get everything done in time." His expression shifted to somber. "The kids are shaken up by Kerry's overdose. I think it was important that an FBI agent came in and warned them about the dangers of drug use." He shook his head. "Kids think they're invincible. Some things never change. Remember those days, Johnny?"

A shadow crossed Johnny's face. The pastor would have had no way of knowing Johnny's tragic upbringing. "I hope we've reached them," Johnny said. "There are some really bad drugs out there. It's no longer an issue of getting high and having a good time. One bad dose and it's all over."

"You'd think the kids would have been scared straight after Peter Heim's death last month. He was by all accounts a good kid, too," the pastor said, threading his fingers in front of him.

"Like you said, a lot of kids think it can't happen to them. Or somehow they're smarter." Johnny glanced around the large gym where the youth had divided up to work on various projects for the fall carnival.

"Let's pray Kerry recovers. Maybe *now* the kids who are inclined to experiment will realize it *could* happen to them."

A young man with a baseball cap on backward approached the pastor. "You got duct tape?" he asked without regard for the adult conversation.

The pastor smiled, lifted the boy's hat off his head and turned it around. "I'm in the middle of a conversation, Sean."

The boy jerked his head back. "Sorry. Just looking for duct tape."

The pastor gestured with his chin toward the corner of the gym. "Look in the box near the door."

"Cool." Sean's sneakers squeaked as he pivoted on the gym floor.

"Kids these days. All about instant gratification." The pastor watched Sean make his way over to the cardboard box in the corner.

"Have you heard any updates about Kerry?" Ellie asked.

The corners of the pastor's mouth tugged down. "No change." He bowed his head reverently. "Our church community is praying for him. His parents are beside themselves. Many families are bringing them meals." He shrugged. "It makes everyone feel like they're doing something when they feel so helpless."

A tinge of bitterness swirled in Ellie's stomach. The church members hadn't come with a parade of meals when her family was going through the biggest nightmare of their lives. *Did they sense Greg's guilt when our family was blinded by his Golden Boy image?*

Ellie wondered if she'd ever get over the sense of betrayal from her brother, one of the few people she truly admired. Looked up to. She glanced away when she felt the first prickles of tears at the backs of her eyes.

"We'll help clean up before we head out," Ellie offered. Some habits died hard.

"Thank you." The pastor turned his attention to Johnny. "Will I see you again? Perhaps at Sunday service?"

Johnny turned to Ellie with a help-me-out-here, wide-eyed gaze.

She smiled, not quite ready to give him an easy out.

"Um…" he muttered.

"Perhaps you'll give it some thought," the pastor said, compassionate to Johnny's discomfort. He lifted an open palm. "I better see that everyone has a project. A lot needs to be done before next weekend." He raised his eyebrows expectantly. "Perhaps you and Agent Rock could find time to join us this week. Many hands make light work."

Ellie sensed Johnny tense next to her. He never came out and said it, but she assumed he wasn't a joiner, and certainly not for a church-related activity.

"I'll see what I can do during the week." She wondered if she'd be able to convince Johnny that reopening her store was a good idea. "I do plan to work the church booth on Saturday night so the kids can enjoy the carnival some."

The pastor patted her elbow. "Excellent. The apple cider is a big seller. See you then. If not sooner." He smiled brightly. "Nice meeting you, Agent Rock. I'll pray that your investigation goes well."

"Thank you," Johnny said.

Ellie walked over to a nearby table and closed the empty doughnut cartons and stacked them one on top of the other. She had decided the best way to get the teenagers to sit and listen to Johnny speak was by bribing them with doughnuts. The smell of chocolate icing and the doughy-fresh doughnuts always reminded her of a simpler time when her family went to church as a family and Ellie's biggest concern was how well she had done on a math test or how long it would take her to write her English essay. Hard to imagine other teenagers had far more pressing concerns than homework.

Johnny walked around the gym gathering up the empty and half-empty foam cups of hot chocolate.

When they met up at the garbage can, Johnny said, "This was a great idea. If we reached one kid, it'll be worth it." There was a wistful quality to his voice that made her respect him even more. This battle, the war on drugs, as the media called it, was personal. He was determined to make a difference and save lives.

Ellie stuffed the empty doughnut boxes into the large gray garbage totes. "I owe you an apology."

Johnny stopped and cocked his head.

"I gave you a lot of grief over arresting my brother. I thought you were wrong. I *did* blame you."

"Your brother is lucky to have you. To have a family that cares." He reached out and slid a strand of her hair through his fingers. When she looked at him with a question in her eyes, he held out his fingers. "Chocolate."

Ellie felt her face heat. "Love me a chocolate doughnut."

Johnny laughed and wiped his fingers on a napkin he snagged from a nearby table.

Ellie lowered her voice. "Why didn't you tell me? Why did you let me believe my brother was innocent?"

Johnny ran a hand across his jaw. "Would you have believed me?"

Ellie bowed her head. Would she have?

"Hey," Johnny said, reaching out and tilting her chin up with his warm finger, "loyalty and loving someone so much that you want to believe the best of them is a good thing." He swallowed hard. "Don't fault yourself for that."

Ellie pulled her sleeves down over her hands. "Do you think my brother is involved now?" The thought of her brother using her shop as a drug drop made her ill.

Johnny touched her hand lightly. "I don't think so, but I do have to consider his history."

Nausea welled up in her throat and she breathed in slowly through her nose. "I pray he's matured since his reckless high school days."

He squeezed her hand, but didn't say anything.

"Thank you for being here." Ellie gazed around the room, hoping to see more garbage she could collect, something to distract her from this intense conversation, a conversation she felt went deeper than her relationship with her brother.

Ellie ducked away from Johnny and grabbed a wet rag from the utility sink in the corner of the gym and wrung it out. She wiped down the two tables and paused. "I hate to think any of these kids are involved with drugs. They seem like such good kids."

"Even good kids can get caught up in drugs. I've seen it too many times to count."

She turned around to face Johnny. Something dark swept across his face. "I'm sorry about your mom."

A half smile tilted the corner of his lips. "Unfortunately my story isn't unique."

Ellie stopped wiping the table and touched his forearm. "You're a good man."

He patted the back of her hand. "You hardly know me."

She shrugged, unable to articulate what she really wanted to say. Something along the lines of, "That may be true, but I like what I see, anyway." She rinsed and wrung the rag in the sink and spread it out on the edge to dry. "I think we've put everything back in its place. The kids can take care of the rest."

"How long have you belonged to this church? You seem at home here." The sincerity in Johnny's question piqued her interest.

Ellie gave his question some thought. "Yeah, I guess I do. It's like a second home. My family has belonged to this church since I was a little girl." She paused. "Of course, I was away for a few years, but when I broke up with my boyfriend and moved back home, this was…well, also part of my coming home." She looked up and flushed when she found him watching her. "Does that fall under TMI?" She giggled nervously.

His unwavering attention made her flush. "Too much information? No, I like learning more about you."

Ellie glanced down at the hardwood floor and the solid red line of the basketball court. "Um, do you belong to a church?"

"No, I don't. Mom worshipped at the altar of drugs."

Something akin to regret welled in her gut. Their conversation had gone from sweet and lighthearted to suddenly dark. She swallowed hard. "I'm sorry." She didn't know what else to say.

He held up his hand. "Nothing for you to be sorry about. My mom made her own choices. Most of them bad." He pulled up the lining of the full garbage can. "Because of her, I am what I am today."

Ellie watched as he tied the bag closed. "We can take that to the Dumpster on our way out."

She walked ahead and held the door open for Johnny. They had spent a lot of time together recently and she had grown to enjoy his company. She did feel a little guilty about keeping him from helping his grandfather pack up the home on Treehaven. However, by Johnny's account, his grandfather didn't seem in much of a rush.

Johnny and Ellie strolled across the parking lot. The light from the lampposts reflected in the rain puddles. The fall air had turned crisp and Ellie zipped up her fleece jacket. Soon, fleece wouldn't cut it and she'd have to break out her thick winter jacket and a knit hat. She wasn't looking forward to that. She never had.

Johnny hoisted the garbage bag into the trash and it landed with a wet plop. She scrunched up her nose as the putrid scent of refuse floated out to greet them from the Dumpster. He wiped his hands together as they strolled toward his vehicle.

Ellie slipped her hands into her pockets and waited for Johnny to unlock the car doors. "Do you think any of these kids know who provided Kerry with drugs?"

"Tough to say. But one thing I do know, they wouldn't have approached us in front of their friends. The most I can hope for is that they took my business card and will call me directly. Anonymously, even."

The sound of shoes running on pavement sent goose bumps racing across Ellie's arms. She spun around, bracing herself. Johnny was at her side in a heartbeat. He discreetly ushered her behind him with one hand and had his other hand under his jacket, no doubt reaching for his gun.

They were in a church parking lot. Wasn't he overreacting a bit? Overreacting? Tell that to her racing heart. Ellie set her shoulders back while her eyes strained to see who was approaching out of the shadows.

"Agent Rock?" The young girl's anguished face became visible under the light of the lamppost.

Ellie stepped around Johnny, relief now pulsing through her veins.

"Kaylee?" Her voice came out high-pitched and squeaky, a result of being startled. The teenager had been in one of the art classes she'd offered as part of her ministry at church. "Is everything okay?" Ellie scanned the parking lot. "Is something wrong?"

Kaylee smiled; a tentative smile, not the genuine smile of a teenager gathered around her friends, laughing at a joke or smiling, trying to get the attention of a young man. No, Kaylee was definitely not herself.

"Um…" Kaylee glanced around, much as Ellie had done. She took a few deep breaths.

Johnny stepped forward, relaxing his protective stance. "Did you need to talk in private?"

Kaylee shook her head, her blunt-cut bob framing her face. "I'm worried about my boyfriend."

Ellie stepped forward and touched the young girl's arm. "What's going on?"

Kaylee's eyes flicked to Johnny, then back to Ellie. "Things were going great until the end of the summer. Then he got distant."

"You guys are young. Maybe he didn't want a girlfriend his senior year."

Ellie cut Johnny a sideways glance at his frank comment. Could he be any more insensitive?

"What Johnny meant…" Ellie attempted to soften his comment when Kaylee held up her hand.

"It's okay. That's what I thought and I was, like, whatever." Kaylee wiped a tear from her eye. "But then I started seeing him around school. Well, when he bothered to show up. At the rate he's going, he won't graduate with the rest of us next spring."

"Are you worried he might be involved with drugs?" There had to be a reason Kaylee had come to them with her concerns. Johnny had just spoken to them about the dangers of drugs and how they needed to reach out to an adult if they had concerns.

Kaylee lifted her shoulders and let them drop.

"Do you want us to talk to him?" Ellie asked.

Indecision creased the young girl's forehead. She tugged at her T-shirt. "Maybe you can stop by his house. Talk to him." She shuffled her feet. "Without him, like, knowing I told you."

"Maybe we can talk to his parents," Johnny said, a question in his voice.

The whites of Kaylee's eyes glinted under the lamppost. "His dad left his mom a few months ago. His mom works all the time. And when she's not working, she sleeps."

There was a slight pause before Johnny said, "What's his name and address? I'll stop by and talk to him."

Kaylee rattled off her boyfriend's information, relief evident in her posture. "Don't tell him I sent you, okay? He'd be really mad."

* * *

"I'll take you home first." Johnny pulled onto the main road, his focus on the yellow paved line illuminated in his headlights. He wanted to put off seeing this Collin kid, Kaylee's boyfriend, but something told him he should reach out to him tonight.

If only someone had reached out to my mother in time…

Ellie shifted in her seat. "No, I want to go, too. He's more likely to talk to me. I know him from our church. Collin's one of the kids who helped me paint the shop. With Kerry."

She let that little nugget hang out there. Collin and Kerry—the young man who was clinging to life after an overdose—were friends.

"He trusts me." Her voice turned shaky. "I have a hard time believing this kid is caught up in drugs." She tugged on her seat belt. "I wouldn't have pegged Kerry for using, either." She sighed heavily as if to say, "What do I know?"

"Even good kids make bad decisions." Johnny scratched his head. "I have to take you home. I can't put you in danger."

Ellie groaned. "Danger? He's a seventeen-year-old kid. A kid I know. He's not going to hurt me."

He shook his head, deciding not to fill her in on his experience with violent kids far younger than seventeen.

Apparently sensing her misstep, Ellie said, "Please. If you sense any danger, I'll go back to the car. Lock myself inside."

The image of shattering glass from the other night scraped across his brain. Locked in his car wasn't exactly Fort Knox. Johnny sagged into the seat and slowed at the stop sign. Collin lived in the trailer park on the other side of town. A sense of urgency made his leg twitch.

"Okay." It would save time, but he didn't like it.

A few minutes later they pulled into *Cedar Heights*, a name far too fancy for the ill-tended trailer homes, many with rust stains on their once-white walls and spare car parts decorating their postage stamp–size front lawns. His assessment was overly critical, but he realized he came upon it honestly. It was in a trailer park like this one in a suburb of Buffalo where his mother had hit rock bottom. Even before his mother had met her fate, he'd felt his had been sealed. The kids in school had teased him relentlessly. Trailer-park kids didn't rank high on the popularity scale.

Kids were ruthless.

Drugs even more so.

"Kaylee said he's in number 34—the last one in this row." Leaning forward, Ellie tugged on her seat belt and angled her head to read the numbers—if there were any—on the sides of the trailers. "There it is." Just as Kaylee had said—the last one.

Johnny slammed his car into Park and grabbed Ellie's hand as she pulled the door release. She smiled up at him under the dome light, understanding in her eyes. "Anything weird, I get back in the car and lock the doors."

Johnny gave her a curt nod.

He walked around and met her by the front of the car. They headed toward the metal platform that served as the front stoop. Just as Ellie's foot hit the first step, Johnny noticed a handlebar poking out from the side of the trailer. He gently touched the small of her back and whispered, "Look." Grabbing her hand, he led her to a motorcycle. Ellie glanced up at him, an expression of shock moving across her face.

"Do you think…?" she whispered, glancing over her shoulder toward the stoop.

"I never got a good look at the make and model of the motorcycle, so maybe it's a coincidence."

The front porch light flipped on, making them both spin around.

A young man Johnny assumed was Collin pushed open the screen door and dragged his hand across his mussed hair. "Hey, get away from my bike." He blinked a few times and his features seemed to soften a bit when he recognized Ellie.

He coughed in his hand and cocked his head. "What are you doing here, Miss Ellie?"

Ellie let go of Johnny's hand and stepped forward, even though Johnny had the gut feeling he should stand in front of her, protect her. "We wanted to check on you. We heard Kerry's in the hospital."

Collin twitched and scrubbed a hand across his face as if they had woken him. "Kerry's messed up."

"How are you doing?"

Collin crossed his arms and rolled up on the balls of his feet. The crickets filled the silence.

Johnny finally spoke. "This your bike?"

"Who's asking?"

"This is my friend, Johnny Rock." Ellie spoke up before he had a chance to.

"What's it to you?" Collin braced his hands on the metal railing and glanced over his shoulder at the front door.

This boy was hiding something.

Johnny stepped forward, his nerve endings on high alert. "I'm Special Agent John Rock of the FBI. Is this your motorcycle?"

The boy's gaze swung to the bike, then to the darkened road. As if on a springboard, he vaulted down the steps and sprinted between the trailers.

Ellie gasped.

Johnny groaned and took off running. Why did

people think running away from a federal agent was a good idea?

Johnny bolted between the trailers, his eyes adjusting to the heavy shadows. He slowed as he approached the corner of the trailer and listened.

Nothing.

He grabbed his gun from his shoulder holster and eased closer to the side of the trailer. When he reached the corner, he stuck close to the cover of the building and sneaked a peek. Collin was crouched down, looking as if he was ready to tackle Johnny if he had blindly chased the kid.

Not a bad idea, kid, *if* he hadn't been a federal agent who knew better.

Johnny pivoted around the corner, his gun aimed at the crouching teen. "Don't move."

"Don't shoot him!"

Ellie blinked a few times, her eyes adjusting to the darkness. Adrenaline made her blood run cold. Johnny had his gun trained on a hunkering Collin. The boy had his hands up, but seemed frozen in an awkward position. In the moonlight, terror glinted in his eyes.

"I'm not going to shoot the kid," Johnny said, a mix of frustration and disgust lacing his voice. He tucked his gun in its holster. "But I don't like surprises. If I had run around this corner, your friend Collin here would have tackled me."

Without the gun aimed at his head, Collin stood and seemed to regain some of his swagger. "Why did you pull a gun on me?" The tone suggested Collin might actually have had the nerve to call Special Agent Johnny Rock "dude," but somewhere deep down the young man had mustered some of the manners Ellie knew he had been taught, and refrained.

"Why did you run from me?" Johnny widened his stance, ready to take on Collin if necessary.

Ellie's pulse thrummed in her ears. Now what had Collin gotten himself involved with?

Collin's shoulders sagged and he sat on a beat-up wicker chair, perched precariously on uneven aqua indoor-outdoor carpeting. His body folded like a crushed pizza box and he jammed his hands into his unruly hair. To Ellie's surprise, his shoulders began to shake. Was he crying?

An outdoor spotlight flicked on and a sharp pain jabbed her in the eyes. The harsh light illuminated the yard, unmasking its truly depressing state of disrepair. A broken umbrella stood sentinel over a worn picnic table. Collin, a boy whose preschool Sunday school class she had assisted, sat broken and confused, on the cusp of being a man, but obviously not ready to step with both feet into the adult world. A shadow crossed the window below the spotlight and Ellie knew her opportunity to talk to Collin was fleeting.

Ellie crouched beside Collin and placed her hands on the arm of the wicker chair. A broken piece of wicker pricked her finger. "What is it, Collin?"

He looked up, his face tearstained. "I didn't mean for you to get hurt. It was just a BB gun."

Ellie slowly stood, a cold chill skittering down her spine. An understanding stretched between her and Johnny. She swallowed hard. "What did you do, Collin?" Her voice held a distant quality, as if she were outside herself watching the situation.

"What's going on out here?" A brassy-voiced, disheveled woman shouted at them as she stormed around the side of the trailer. Ellie barely recognized her as the young mother, lines creasing her eyes and mouth, who used to show up in church with her husband and son in a neat sweater set. That all seemed a million years ago.

"I'm sorry, Mom." The pain in Collin's eyes broke Ellie's heart.

Anger and confusion fought for dominance on Mrs. Parker's tired face. "Who...?" Her tone was uncertain. "What's going on?"

Johnny was the first to speak. "I'm Special Agent John Rock. I'd like to talk to your son if I can."

Mrs. Parker rubbed her eyes and tried to muster some of the anger that had brought her storming outside only moments ago. "Does he need a lawyer?" Her voice shook. "I can't afford a lawyer."

"I need to tell them," Collin said, sounding more like a little boy than a teenager. "I need to shake this guilt. I can't stand it anymore." He looked up at his mother with all the conflicting emotions of a son who was about to come clean and accept his punishment.

This was the same young man who, when he was just a boy, had cried when he'd skinned his knee on the playground and clung to Ellie's waist. Ellie was like a big sister to a lot of these kids. Something in her heart shifted. Anyone—*anyone*—could take a step off the right path and land in a world of hurt. If she had learned anything today, it was that stark reality.

"We want to help your son, Mrs. Parker, before something happens that can't be reversed." Ellie placed her hand on the woman's crossed forearm. Mrs. Parker looked as though she wanted to run like her son, but instead, she slowly sat in the chair next to Collin's. Her chair wobbled on the uneven earth as she leaned to clutch his hand. "What did you do?"

"I took the BB gun Dad gave me and shot out a window on Main Street."

Ellie's stomach hollowed out. A million thoughts

shifted through her brain, none of them making sense. Collin Parker had shot at her.

"I didn't know you'd be there. I thought the store was closed…" His voice shook. "All the other stores were closed. And it was dark." He scrubbed his hand across his face and his whole body shuddered as if he had tasted something sour. "I didn't mean to hurt anyone."

Ellie was only vaguely aware of Johnny making a phone call over the sounds of Collin's sobs and Mrs. Parker's quiet questions. "Why would you do that? What were you possibly thinking?"

Collin stood and his mother rose along with him. He grabbed his mother's wrists and flung her away from him. She stumbled back and turned her ankle. Johnny steadied her. "Easy, Collin." Then to Mrs. Parker, "Are you okay?"

She nodded; a confused look in her eyes. She seemed to have aged beyond her years. The cigarette lines around her eyes and mouth didn't help. "Collin needs his father. He ran off with that—" Her face crumpled in distaste as she struggled to get the right word out. "He hasn't been the same since his dad left. We had to move here." She held up her hand to the trailer. "He's hanging around the wrong people." She looked at Johnny, imploring him with her eyes. "You can't hold him responsible."

"How old is your son?" Johnny asked.

"Seventeen."

"I've called the police. They'll be here soon to take Collin in and question him," Johnny said.

Panic lit Collin's features and he bounced on the balls of his feet. "I can't go to jail." In an explosion of energy, Collin bolted. This time Johnny was faster. He stepped in front of the boy and blocked him with a shot to the chest with his shoulder.

"You have to stop doing that." Johnny gritted his teeth and spun Collin around, yanking his arms behind him. "I didn't want to do this."

Ellie winced as Johnny snapped handcuffs onto Collin's wrists.

Mrs. Parker paced the small space. The spotlight highlighted a face filled with regret. "It's all my fault."

Ellie reached out, but Mrs. Parker jerked away.

Johnny shoved Collin down on the picnic bench. "Hang tight. Officer Bailey's on his way."

Ellie brushed past Mrs. Parker, who stood with her arms wrapped around her middle as she rocked back and forth. "Collin—" Ellie envisioned the little boy who couldn't sit still during Bible study "—why did you shoot the front of my shop?"

Collin lifted his shoulders and wiped his nose on the sleeve of his T-shirt. "Some guy paid us. I needed the money."

"What are you talking about?" Mrs. Parker pushed Ellie out of the way so she could get in Collin's face.

"I needed the money. Okay? I *needed* it!" Collin's words exploded, spittle flying from his mouth. "It's not like you're going to give me any money. You're always complaining you don't have any." He scrunched up his nose as he threw a disgusted look at the trailer he called home. Then, as if contrition had slammed into him, he bowed his head. "I'm sorry, Mom. I'm really sorry." He shifted awkwardly and pleaded to Johnny, "I can't go to prison. I can't. I'll die there."

Ellie took a chance, wrapped her arm around Mrs. Parker's shoulders and guided her away from her raging son.

Mrs. Parker wiped at the tears streaming down her face. "I should have done a better job. I let my son down."

Ellie made shushing sounds, her heart racing in her ears. Her mouth had gone dry.

Johnny placed his hand on Collin's shoulder. "Who paid you to shoot out the front of Ellie's shop?"

Collin hung his head. "The guy paid Kerry. He said he had to make it look like he was going after Ellie." The words rushed out. "Kerry wasn't feeling good, so he talked me into it. Gave me fifty bucks. I thought it was no big deal. A broken window. Nothing more. I was so pumped up on adrenaline I couldn't think straight even when I noticed someone standing near the door. *You* weren't supposed to be there."

His last sentence pointed the blame at Ellie and she bit back her anger.

"Kerry…?" Kerry who had overdosed. Pinpricks washed over Ellie and she started to tremble.

Collin shook his head, a pitiful look on his young face.

"What's the guy's name? The one who paid Kerry?" Johnny asked.

Collin shook his head. "Kerry never told me."

Ellie's heart sunk. Now Kerry was in a coma. Clinging to life.

They might never find out who had paid Kerry to shoot her window out.

EIGHT

"You can't stay alone in the garage apartment. You're not safe there." Outside the police station, Johnny closed Ellie's passenger door and watched as she collapsed into the seat and brushed a strand of hair out of her face. He had encouraged her to leave the apartment before, but this time he wasn't taking no for an answer.

He walked around to the driver's side and climbed in. She turned in her seat while she snapped her seat belt into place. "You're not suggesting I get a roommate."

He tapped on the steering wheel. "Maybe you should move into the main house with your mom."

Ellie held up her hands in a hold-on-a-minute gesture. "I've been working hard to be on my own." She frowned. "Not that living in a garage apartment next to my childhood home is some huge leap, but it's a start." She shook her head, the fight seeming to drain from her.

"I don't want you to be alone." Johnny shifted the car into Drive and waited for a squad car to pass in the police station parking lot.

"I still can't believe Collin shot out the windows of my shop." Her voice shook, partly from fear, partly from betrayal. Until Kerry woke up—if Kerry woke up—they might not know who'd paid him to do it.

"How much danger do you really think I'm in?" Her face turned ashen. "Collin said Kerry gave him strict instructions to vandalize my shop when no one was around. Maybe I'm okay..." Her voice trailed off.

"Collin isn't a reliable witness. He's a kid with a drug problem and desperate for money. I don't think he's going to confess to anything more than he did. Nor is he going to rat out his best friend." He covered her hand with his. Hers was freezing. "Someone paid Kerry to scare you. Even if Kerry's in a coma and Collin's in jail, the person we really need to worry about is still out there. He'll find another impressionable kid to hire to scare you." *Or worse.*

Ellie let out a loud huff. "If I'm in danger, I can't move into my mom's house. I don't want to bring danger to her doorstep." Ellie's voice grew quiet. "She's been through enough over the years."

Johnny squeezed her hand. "Then move in with me."

Ellie coughed out her surprise. "Excuse me."

"Move into my grandfather's house. This way I can protect you."

Ellie leaned back into her car seat. "Really? Oh, man," she said, as if now just realizing something. "I'm the victim, yet I'm the prisoner. I have to leave my apartment. I have to close my shop."

"It may feel that way, but it's only temporary."

Ellie glanced down at her hands. "What if you can't find whoever is behind this?"

"I will."

She met his gaze.

"You realize I can't make you do anything. I can't make you leave your apartment."

"But you'd like me to…" She stated the obvious, the sound of defeat in her voice.

Johnny ran a hand over his whiskered jaw, considering something. "Maybe we're going about this all wrong. Last solid lead we had was a package shipped to Gifts and More's address."

Ellie jerked her head back, following his train of thought. "So now you *want* me to stay open?"

"I could help you unpack the rest of the boxes. Do odd jobs around the store during business hours. Be there to protect you."

A thin line creased Ellie's forehead. "You want to work for me?"

"Not exactly." He laughed. "I'll help. Free of charge."

"Won't whoever had the drugs shipped to my store's address get suspicious? That an FBI agent is now working in the store?"

"Maybe, but perhaps things are already in play. Things they won't be able to stop. Like additional shipments. Or threats to you. I don't want you in there by yourself."

Ellie's heavy sigh filled the quiet space. "What about your grandfather? Doesn't he need your help getting the house on Treehaven ready to sell?"

"He won't mind the delay."

Ellie ran her hands up and down the thighs of her jeans. "When you started this investigation, did you really think I had something to do with the drugs?"

Johnny searched her eyes, hoping she'd understand. "In the beginning, I had to consider all angles."

"And you already knew what my brother was capable of." Her voice grew quiet. "You've also been investigating my brother…" She watched his face and he did his best to not show emotion. "Greg's been helping me some in the shop. Do you think…?" He detected fear in her question.

"Like I told you before, I have no leads indicating your brother is involved."

Ellie bit her bottom lip. "This is all so unbelievable."

Johnny decided he needed to be honest with

Ellie if he hoped to gain her trust. "I've also been tracking Roger Petersen. I don't have anything on him. Yet." Roger rubbed him the wrong way. Johnny thrummed his fingers on the steering wheel. "Our best hope is to find out who paid Kerry and Collin to shoot out the shop windows. Go from there."

"Yeah." Ellie didn't sound optimistic.

Johnny flipped the directional to turn down her street. "Let's grab a few things from your apartment and then I'm taking you to my grandfather's house."

"This will go over like a lead balloon with my mother."

"Wait here." The bottom step creaked as Ellie spun around. For appearances' sake, she didn't want to make a habit of inviting him up to her apartment. Johnny hesitated, his hand on the railing. A look she couldn't quite discern washed across his face. "Is there a back entrance to your place?"

Ellie's stomach dropped. "No, only this one staircase." She tapped her palm on the wooden railing, mustering a confidence she didn't feel.

"I'll be fine." She was starting to wonder if that was her brain or her exhaustion talking. "Wait right here. I'll leave the door ajar. I'll talk to you the whole time." She angled her head and gave him her best this-is-how-it's-going-to-be-whether-you-like-it-or-not look. The one she had seen her mother use a million times to great effect.

She spun on her heel, not waiting around for him to argue. She reached the top landing and hollered over her shoulder, "I'll hurry."

Mentally figuring out what she had to pack and wondering for how long—surely he'd let her come back to her apartment for more things—she fumbled in her purse for the keys. Finally she found them at the bottom next to six pens and a wadded-up grocery list. She really needed to clean out her purse.

She lifted the key to the bright pink door, her statement piece on her boring apartment, and her stomach dropped to her shoes. With a shaky hand, she pushed the door. It swung open.

Swallowing around a hard lump, she flattened herself against the dusty outside wall. At the bottom of the steps with his back to her, Johnny scanned the yard. She glanced back at the door. It yawned open about a foot. It *hadn't* been locked.

"Johnny..." Her shaky voice trailed off.

He slowly turned around. The look on her face must have said everything she couldn't. He took the stairs two at a time. When he reached her side, he silently placed a hand on her arm. "Stay here," he mouthed. Gun drawn, Johnny entered the apartment.

Her heart beat wildly in her ears, drowning out the crickets and any sound of Johnny...or an intruder. She wondered if she should run for his car and lock herself in, but she didn't have his keys.

The fine hairs on the back of her neck prickled to life. She felt exposed, vulnerable, afraid. A soft touch to her arm made her jump. She spun around. Johnny's curious expression locked on her. He cocked his head toward the door. "It's all clear."

Knees trembling, Ellie leaned back on the rough siding on the exterior of the garage. A sharp corner of siding dug into her back. She pushed away and turned to go into her apartment. She stepped through the door. Everything she owned was scattered around her apartment. Confusion swirled in her head.

"I never thought..."

"They'd come to your home?" Johnny finished her thought.

"Yes. I considered this my sanctuary."

Her face must have showed every emotion in her heart because Johnny gently touched her arm and guided her to the couch. "Whoever was here is gone." He pushed aside a pile of books on her coffee table and sat in front of her. "I'm sorry you have to go through this."

Ellie scanned her small apartment. The one closet was open and everything had been thrown out. All the drawers in her dresser and china cabinet were either half-open or had been pulled out all together. "What's going on?"

"Whoever is dealing drugs thinks you stole the shipment. They couldn't find it in your shop, so—"

"They decided to search my home."

Ellie bowed her head and rested her forehead in the palm of her hand. A sick feeling made her dinner roil in her stomach. She doubted she'd ever be able to eat a chicken panini again. She groaned, not knowing what to say.

"We need to notify the police and get you to safety."

Ellie nodded and stood, her legs weak underneath her.

"Don't touch anything. Grab the basics. We'll wait and talk to the police and let them investigate the scene."

She looked up at Johnny, who seemed to be blocking her view of something. "Come on, let's wait outside." His rush to get her outside agitated her.

What was he hiding?

She cut him a sideways glance then moved toward the wall. She started to hyperventilate and the world narrowed to a dark-walled tunnel. Next to an oil painting of the skyline of Buffalo— one she had painted on a glorious fall day from the marina—was a photo of her with Greg and Johnny from Johnny's so-called high school days.

Ellie remembered the exact day. Her mother had found out it was Johnny's birthday and had insisted on baking him a cake. The three of them were gathered around the cake, a genuine smile on Johnny's face.

Ellie blinked away the memory and struggled to focus.

Smack-dab in the middle of her face in the photo was a knife.

Ellie slowly turned around, terror pulsing through her veins.

Johnny's gaze grew intense. "We need to go outside. *Now.*"

"Wait. Wait." Ellie grabbed at Johnny's arm as they hustled to his car in the driveway. Adrenaline flooded her system not allowing her to think straight. "I can't leave my mother."

Johnny grabbed her small overnight bag and tossed it into the backseat of his car and slammed the door. "We have to wait for the police." He jammed his fingers through his mussed hair. "Let's get your mom while we wait. Do you think she'll go with us?"

Ellie laughed; a brittle sound considering the circumstances. "Maybe we can talk her into going to Greg's house for a little while." She strode to the front door and turned the handle. And, as always, the door swung open.

"Doesn't your mom lock the house?"

"Only at night when she sleeps."

Johnny frowned.

"We live in a small town."

He opened his mouth about to say something when Ellie interrupted, "*Yes*, I locked the door to my apartment."

His mouth slanted into a half grin. "Already reading my mind?"

Ellie rolled her eyes and stepped into the small entryway and called out to her mother so as not to startle her. The only reply was the sound of laugh tracks and the familiar blue flicker of the television in the darkened living room.

She strode into the living room and found her mother, head tipped back, her feet propped up on the extended recliner. "Mom," she called in a loud whisper.

Nancy Winters's mouth snapped shut and she abruptly sat forward. Her displeasure was immediately evident on the strained set of her mouth.

"What? What is it?"

"Someone broke into my apartment."

"What? When?" Her mother grabbed the handle on the recliner and snapped the footrest closed. "How can that be? I've been home all night."

"Did you see anyone?" Johnny asked. "Hear anything?"

"Of course I didn't see anyone. If I'd seen someone, I would have called the police." Nancy pushed to her feet and wrung her hands. "Why is it that there's always trouble when you're around?" She glared at Johnny, her nerves getting the best of her.

"Mom." Ellie put her hand on her mother's forearm. For the first time she understood how wrong her family had been for blaming Johnny for Greg's mistakes.

But that was Greg's story to tell.

"We need to stay somewhere else until Johnny catches the guy who's harassing me."

Her mother lowered herself onto the arm of the recliner. "I'm not going anywhere."

"It's not forever. Just till some arrests are made," Ellie said, trying to convince her mother.

"Where will I go?" Worry flitted across her mother's face. For nearly sixty, her mother had a youthful appearance, but she had aged since Ellie's father had died.

"I'll call Greg. I'm sure he wouldn't mind your sleeping in the extra room, like you did when Grace was born and they needed help."

Nancy ran her hand down the worn corduroy

on the back of the recliner. "*I'll* call him." Her tone had a possessive quality to it.

The sound of the front door opening caught their attention. Johnny held up his arm in a protective gesture. "Stay here."

"Mom?" Greg called out.

Ellie's older brother stepped into the family room, a confused look on his face. "Is everything okay?"

Her mother ran over and hugged Greg. "Someone broke into Ellie's apartment." Her mother pulled away and crossed her arms. "Johnny thinks I'd be safer staying at your place until they make an arrest."

Greg blinked a few times. "Of course." He sounded uncertain. "Grace would love to have you stay."

Nancy stepped away from her son and smoothed a hand down her shirt. "I suppose I should pack a few things." She shook her head and turned to go pack.

Johnny crossed his arms over his broad chest. "What made you stop by your mother's so late?"

The tone of Johnny's question made Ellie's heart sink. She closed her eyes briefly and said a silent prayer. *Please, Lord, don't let Greg be involved with this mess. Not again.*

Greg lifted his hand; a plastic bag dangled

from his fingers. "Leftovers from the party. Mom forgot to grab them when she left."

Johnny nodded, as if satisfied. "Take your mom to your house and keep an eye on her. Ellie will stay at my grandfather's house."

"Ellie, there's room at my house for you," Greg said, his tone flat.

Ellie rubbed her forearms. "I think it would be better for everyone if I stayed away from my family. I don't want to bring anyone else into this mess."

Greg nodded, an uncertain look in his eyes.

Ellie glanced toward the back hall where their mother had disappeared. "You really should talk to Mom. Tell her the truth."

Greg bowed his head, all the years of guilt and secrets weighing on him. "I will."

Flashing lights flooded into the kitchen. Johnny touched Ellie's arm. "The police are here."

Ellie nodded. She turned to Greg. "Make sure mom is safe."

"I will."

Ellie studied her brother's face. Did she really know him?

NINE

The next morning, Johnny wiped the sweat that was dripping into his eyes as he ran up the final incline toward his grandfather's Victorian home. The temperature was barely in the sixties, but he had worked up a sweat jogging. He turned up the driveway and the hexagonal structure on the second story of the home stood prominently over the large yard.

Johnny planted his hands on his waist and bent over, dragging in huge breaths. *No more skipping my daily routine.* It didn't take long to get out of shape.

When he was a little kid, his mother had bemoaned her miserable youth. Her miserable parents. Her woe-is-me childhood.

His grandfather. This house. Everything about Williamstown…contradicted his mother's tales of gloom.

It was only after his grandfather had allowed him to move in when he was in his early twenties that he had learned that his mother's bedroom had been in the third-story alcove, a round bedroom with windows on four sides. A part of him had felt betrayed. She had portrayed her childhood as far different. He had to reframe the past that his mother had lied about.

The trill of his cell phone snapped him out of his reverie. He stood straight and pulled it out of his running jacket. The Caller ID read Williamstown PD. He snapped it open. "Rock."

"Why do I feel like saying 'paper, scissors'?" There was no mistaking the sarcastic tone of Officer Bailey.

Not exactly in the mood, Johnny said curtly, "What's going on?"

"Kerry Pitz. The kid who nearly overdosed?"

"Yeah." His pulse *whoosh-whoosh-whoosh*ed in his ears.

"He's awake."

Johnny grabbed the corner of his shirt and wiped the sweat off his brow. Optimism lifted his mood. "You talk to him?"

"Parents are closing ranks. You know how it is with kids and their rich parents. It's all 'not my child.' They can't see past their white picket fences and fancy cars."

Johnny raised his eyes to the stately home. Was that what had happened with his grandparents? Blind to their own daughter's problems? Unwilling to recognize the depths of their daughter's drug problem until it was too late?

"We need to find out what he knows. We need to talk to him before the hospital releases him. Before someone gets to him. See if he can give us the name of the guy who paid him and Collin to bust out the windows of Gifts and More.

"Do you think he's in danger? Can you spare an officer to sit outside his room?" The flutter of the lacy window curtains on the second story caught Johnny's attention as a long sigh stretched across the line.

"We're a small-town operation. We don't have the resources for babysitting."

Johnny made a noncommittal sound at the back of his throat as he stared at his grandfather's house.

The white trim on the windows needed painting. A pang of guilt poked him. His grandfather couldn't keep up this place, yet he truly didn't want to sell. He shook away his train of thought. Neither Johnny nor his grandfather had any business taking care of an old Victorian. Sell it and turn it over to some young, ambitious couple. People were always looking to do that today. Buy a fixer-upper.

"I have an idea," Bailey said as Johnny's focus was drawn to the window where Ellie suddenly appeared, unaware of him watching her from the driveway. Her focus was beyond him. Down the road. The unguarded look on her face exposed raw emotion, making him feel as though he had intruded on a private moment.

Didn't Ellie know the Pitz family from church?

"Care to tell me or would you rather just keep me in the dark?" Johnny imagined Officer Bailey scrunching up his face.

"I'll keep you in the loop. Let me get things lined up."

Johnny paced the top of the driveway to cool down from his run. "Any info on the break-in last night at Ellie's?"

"Nothing. Guy must have been wearing gloves. I'll let you know if we find anything."

"Thanks." Johnny ended the call and stuffed the phone into his pocket. He went around back and let himself in through the French doors, the same way he had left. Duke looked up, then put his head back down between his paws, as if to say, "Oh, it's only you."

Johnny took the back stairs two at a time. He lifted his hand to knock on the guest room door when it flew open. Ellie stood there in a University at Buffalo sweatshirt and Cookie Monster PJ bottoms. Her pink lips formed an unspoken *Oh*.

Johnny took a step back. "Sorry, didn't mean to startle you."

Her gaze traveled the length of him. "You've

already been out for a run. What time is it?" She glanced over her shoulder, as if to find the answer somewhere in the guest room.

"It's a little after eight."

"Oh."

"I got a call from Officer Bailey."

"Any news on the break-in?" Alarm threaded through her voice.

"No, sorry. It's Kerry. Kerry Pitz. He's awake."

Her fingers fluttered at the base of her neck. "Did he tell anyone who paid him and Collin to shoot out my shop's window?"

"No. I was hoping you'd be up for a little trip to the hospital. To talk to Kerry. His parents are stalling the police. They won't be able to do that forever, but out of respect for his father—a well-respected lawyer—they don't want to push it."

"But you think they'll let me in."

He cocked his head. "It's worth a try."

Ellie bit her bottom lip. "Do you think we have time to go to church service this morning?"

Johnny studied the floor for a moment, then lifted his gaze to meet hers. "Let me make a few calls. I want to make sure Kerry doesn't get discharged before we get there."

Immediately after church, Ellie found herself in the waiting room of the north wing of the small community hospital. As Ellie understood it, there had been discussions about moving Kerry to a larger health-care facility in Buffalo once his condition stabilized. Then Kerry had proved them all wrong by waking up.

Ellie touched Mrs. Pitz's cold hand; her boneless frame slouched in an orange vinyl chair from the height of the disco era. "Mrs. Pitz?"

Mrs. Pitz sniffed and sunk further into the chair, if that were possible. The woman here was a far cry from the chatty young mother who used to pick Kerry up from Sunday-school class all those years ago.

"Mrs. Pitz, we'd like to talk to your son if that's okay with you."

Mrs. Pitz nodded and ran a hand under her nose. "I'm having a hard time processing this all." Her voice trembled. "But if he has information that can spare some other family this nightmare…" Her voice waned.

Johnny gave her a brief nod. "Kerry is eighteen, but you're welcome to come in the room with us. Be with your son." They had decided to ask his mother permission to talk to Kerry even though he was an adult and allowed to make his own decisions. They figured getting buy-in from the parents would fuel their success.

Mrs. Pitz held up a shaky hand. "No, go on in. I'll be out here." Her forced smile didn't reach her sad eyes. Perhaps she was afraid to hear what her son had to say. Or perhaps she was more afraid of what her husband would say when he returned and learned she had allowed an FBI agent to speak to their son.

Johnny tipped his head toward the door.

Ellie led the way into the private room then leaned toward Johnny. "His father's a lawyer. I don't think he'd want us in here."

There was some cartoon show on the television but Kerry's eyes were staring at the white wall.

"Kerry," Ellie called softly. The young man slowly turned his head, his thick black locks splayed on the stark white pillowcase. "How are you?"

"Been better." His attention shifted to the lump created by his feet under the thin white bedspread.

Slowly, Kerry glanced at Johnny. "Who's he?"

"Special Agent Johnny Rock with the FBI." Ellie wrapped her hands around the cool bar at the foot of the bed. She held her breath, waiting for his response.

Kerry rolled his eyes and then winced, as if the effort hurt his head. "It would have been better if I'd died."

"Please, don't say that. Your parents would have been heartbroken."

He rubbed a hand with tubes coming out of it

across his forehead. "They're already heartbroken. I'm every parent's worst nightmare."

"You made a huge mistake, but you're alive."

Kerry stared at her, the hurt apparent in his eyes. "Why are you here?" he asked Johnny.

Ellie moved to the side of his bed. "Collin shot a BB through my shop's window."

Something akin to surprise flashed in his eyes before he caught himself. "And…?"

"He told us someone paid you to do it."

"Collin talks a lot." Kerry aimed the remote control at the television and turned it off. "Nothing but junk on during the day. How do people stand it?"

He dropped the remote next to him on the bed and studied the tubes coming out of the back of his hand. "Anyone get hurt?"

"Not seriously."

Kerry finally lifted his eyes to meet hers. "You're here to find out who paid me."

"Yes," Johnny said, hanging back a bit so as not to intimidate the young man.

"Why would I want to tell law enforcement anything? I'd get myself in trouble. My dad says only fools talk to cops."

"Do you want anyone else to get a dose of those toxic drugs?" The steely intensity in Johnny's words made Ellie wince.

A long silence stretched between them. Then

Kerry swallowed hard before speaking. "My father's going to disown me anyway. I've got nothing to lose…"

Ellie was about to say something reassuring when Kerry continued, "I don't know his name."

Johnny pulled a chair alongside the boy's bed and leaned in conspiratorially. "Can you describe him?"

Kerry traced the buttons on the remote control. "I was supposed to meet my dealer in the park. You know…the park on Glenn Street?"

Johnny nodded, but didn't speak. Neither did Ellie. She feared anything she said would cause him to stop talking. Her mouth grew dry. How had this young man from a great family gotten himself in such a desperate position?

"What happened when you met your dealer in the park?" Johnny encouraged him.

Kerry clenched and unclenched his hands. "A guy…a guy I didn't know strolled up to me. He had on a hoodie and a baseball cap. I could see the whites of his eyes glistening in the light of the lamppost, but I wouldn't recognize him if I saw him again or anything."

The young man twisted the sheets in his tight grip. "I was really nervous because I owed my dealer some money. I thought maybe he'd sent this guy to collect." His face crumbled in distress and his nostrils flared before he seemed to compose himself. "I suppose in a way he had."

"What did this man ask you to do?"

"He gave me some of the stuff and told me it was on him if I could do him a favor." Kerry sniffed. "He told me to break the front window of Gifts and More."

"Kerry, you know that shop is mine. You helped me paint the walls. You've known me since you've been a little kid." A hollowness expanded in Ellie's chest.

Kerry picked at a loose thread on the bedspread. "I know." He sniffed again and his jaw trembled. He looked so much younger than his eighteen years. "No one was supposed to get hurt. I figured a BB gun would do the job without hurting anyone. The guy said to shatter the windows when the shop was closed. He emphasized that part... Collin and I started getting high. Well, actually, I was shooting up. I was so out of it, I talked Collin into doing it. Promised him fifty bucks. I was going to borrow it from my dad."

"Why not just stiff the guy? You already had the drugs."

Kerry slowly shook his head. "I ain't going to borrow more trouble than I already had. I had to shoot out the window. No biggie, right? Besides, my dad would never miss fifty bucks." He laughed; a rueful sound.

"Has Collin come in to see you since you've woken up?"

"No…" He shook his head slowly. "Why?" His mouth gaped open, as if he was about to be sick.

Ellie grabbed a plastic basin and held it near Kerry's chest in case he needed it. He pushed it away. "I'm not going to be sick." He shook his head. "Tell me. What's up with Collin?"

"Ellie and I were standing in the doorway when Collin drove by and shot out the door."

"Idiot," Kerry muttered. "That's not what was supposed to happen." He punched the mattress next to his hip.

"When you decide to get involved with drugs, bad stuff happens." Johnny leaned back in the chair.

"You could have died, Kerry." Ellie's voice was filled with compassion. "If you don't care about yourself, think of your family. Your little brother."

Kerry's mouth pinched. A smattering of peach fuzz covered his unshaved jaw. "I'm so ashamed. Ashamed of what I've become."

Ellie placed a hand on Kerry's shoulder; it felt thin under her touch. He had once been such an athletic, strong kid. She had imagined big things for him.

Drugs only subtracted from a person's life. They had clearly made more than its share of withdrawals from Kerry's.

"Can you tell us anything about the man who asked you to shatter the windows?"

Kerry closed his eyes. The movement under his eyelids suggested he was replaying recent events. "He smelled like my grandma's."

"Your grandma's? Like mothballs?" Ellie prompted, not understanding.

"No." His forehead wrinkled, as though he was slightly annoyed. "My grandma's kitchen. Her house smelled awesome." A dreamy look descended into his eyes. "When she hugged me, even her clothes smelled like cake." A half smile quirked the corner of his mouth.

A cool dread pooled in Ellie's gut. No, no...it couldn't be. She glanced over at Johnny. Was he thinking the same thing she was?

Johnny leaned forward. "Did you notice his shoes?"

Kerry's eyes brightened. "Yes. Yes!" He pointed with his finger. "He had on those high-end shoes with that famous basketball player's name on them. I'm not much into basketball," he said as an aside, "but I've seen them around. Not exactly something I'd wear."

"What color were they?" Ellie asked, anticipation making her scalp prickle.

"Yellow and orange. Ugliest things I've ever seen." Kerry's nose turned up at the memory.

The walls in the sterile room suddenly felt

close. Too close. Ellie didn't dare whisper the name that sprang to mind. Not in front of Kerry.

The young man had described Tony Vino, the baker's son. A flush of dread washed over her. Her best friend's boyfriend.

"I'm taking you to my grandfather's house then I'm going to talk to Tony." Johnny pressed the elevator button—L for lobby—in the three-story, rural hospital. The doors eased closed and the elevator car began its slow decent.

Ellie shook her head. "No, you are *not* going to dump me off at your grandfather's. I want to hear what Tony has to say for himself. He's messing with my livelihood."

"He also might be a drug dealer and a murderer." He turned to face her in the elevator.

"Please don't shut me out."

"A student died from a drug overdose. If Tony's been the one dealing, he could be held accountable for the young man's death."

Frustrated, Johnny turned toward the front of the elevator car, waiting for the door to open.

"My future is at stake," Ellie said, her tone soft and pleading.

Johnny spun around. "My job is to keep you safe."

"I thought your job was to get the drug dealer."

He clenched his jaw. Why did he let this woman get under his skin?

"Yes, my job *is* to get the drug dealer. But my job is also to keep you safe. I need to tuck you somewhere."

Ellie punched the emergency button and the elevator lurched to a stop. "I am not a victim. I'm not going to be tucked anywhere." She jerked her chin up in defiance. "I can help you."

Johnny started to open his mouth to ask her how she planned to do that when Ellie rushed on. "Tony's dating my business partner, Ashley. They spend almost all their free time together. I'll call her and we can pinpoint his location."

It was Johnny's turn to shake his head. "And alert him we're on to him? No way. I'm dropping you off at my grandfather's house and I don't want to hear another word about it." He reached around Ellie and released the emergency stop on the elevator.

When the door finally opened Ellie stormed past him, strode through the lobby and the double doors and out to the parking lot.

He had to walk briskly to catch up to her. "Ellie." She kept walking. "Ellie, wait. Please, stop."

She stopped in her tracks, but didn't turn around.

Johnny jogged to catch up with her. "I only want what's best for you."

She hung her head dramatically. "The story of my life. Everyone always thinks they know what's best for me. When do I get to decide?"

Johnny lifted her chin with a hooked index finger, forcing her to look at him. "Keeping you safe is a lot different than telling you what you can and cannot do, you realize that, right?"

She turned her face and crossed her arms.

"I'd never presume to tell you what to do, but this is important. I want to make sure you're safe." He reached up and touched her forearm. She dropped her arms.

"Okay, take me to your grandfather's." She pointed her finger at his chest. "But you better call me the minute you find Tony. And you need to make sure Ashley's okay."

He guided her by the small of the back to the car. "I will. But you realize I might not have anything to arrest him on. All we have is a smell and a sneaker type."

She nodded. A slow smile formed on her pink lips. "Maybe he'll crack under your intense interrogation." She leaned into him briefly and the fresh scent of her shampoo reached his nose. "I can't believe Kerry and Collin agreed to shoot out my windows. I trusted those boys." Her voice muffled against his shirt.

He dragged his hand down her silky hair to her back. "I'm sorry. It's painful when people you trust let you down." The image of his mother floated to mind.

"I know." Ellie stepped away from him all too soon and reached for the car door.

Johnny held the door as she climbed in. He leaned into the doorway. "You can trust me, Ellie."

A flicker of something he couldn't quite name flashed in her eyes. "I know." She grabbed the seat belt and clicked it into place. "I know."

TEN

A single light illuminated the porch of the old Victorian home when Johnny dropped Ellie off. Slowly, she climbed out of Johnny's car, wishing she could go with him. She wanted to confront Tony herself. Give him a piece of her mind. But she realized personal satisfaction wasn't worth risking the investigation or her well-being.

"Call me after you've found Tony," she said, bending to look at him before closing her door.

Johnny nodded then turned to climb out his side of the car.

"You don't have to walk me to the door."

"What kind of gentleman would I be if I didn't walk you to the door?"

A warm tingling raced through her as they met at the front of his vehicle. He pressed his solid hand against the small of her back. She could get used to this. But did she want to? She had vowed to be independent. Not rely on a man.

But she hadn't intended to meet *this* man. Why

couldn't Johnny Rock have come along a year or so from now, once she had her shop firmly established and her feet back on the ground? An uncomfortable foreboding started working on her. Would she be on solid ground with Gifts and More? Ever?

Johnny opened the front door and they stepped into his grandfather's foyer.

The sound of the clock ticking filled the space, so different from her childhood home where the sound of laugh tracks and obnoxiously loud commercials filled the home 24/7 so that sometimes she couldn't think.

"Thank you for taking me to church this morning," Ellie said, not quite ready to see him leave.

"No problem." Johnny palmed the cap of the newel post. "I haven't seen the inside of a church in a long time."

"Maybe you'll go with me again?" She raised her eyebrows.

Johnny lifted a shoulder noncommittally and changed the subject. "I need to find Tony. While I'm gone—"

"I promise I won't go to the shop or anywhere else someone could find me." Just saying the words out loud made her insides freeze with icy dread.

Then, trying to shake the feeling, she added, "I'll get lost in a book." She nodded toward the library off the foyer. "I'm sure I can find something in there to hold my interest."

Johnny tucked a strand of hair behind her ear. "When this is all over..."

"You'll be back in Buffalo and I'll be struggling to make ends meet in my gift shop." She smiled, but the effort felt strained.

He dragged a thumb across her cheek, leaving tingles in its wake. "I see things going in a different direction."

Ellie wanted to say something cute or sarcastic about how things that were good for her didn't usually work out. But something in his warm gaze kept her quiet, made her think, *Maybe, just maybe*.

A tense charge settled between them. The tick-tock-tick of the grandfather clock grew hushed. The movement of his thumb across her cheek stopped and a tenderness coiled around her heart. He leaned in and brushed a kiss across her lips. She pressed into him and he wrapped his arms around her. His strength, his warmth, his solidness transferred to her, making her feel safe, protected, yet not smothered as she had felt in other relationships.

Maybe, just maybe rang in her head once again.

Johnny kissed her forehead and stepped away. "I'll be back soon." His voice was raspy, husky. A spark lit his eyes. "Don't go anywhere."

Ellie nodded, unable to find the words. What had just happened here?

Johnny slipped out the front door and she closed it behind him, bolting it. Hugging her arms to herself, she turned around and froze. Johnny's grandfather stood at the end of the hallway, Duke at his feet.

"Sorry, I didn't mean to startle you," the older gentleman said.

"It's okay," Ellie said, her hand still pressed to her chest.

"Johnny headed back out?"

"Yeah, he has a lead in the case."

Buddy shook his head and turned toward the kitchen. Ellie followed him. He filled Duke's food and water bowls while she watched him from a stool at the island. His grandfather started talking without looking at her, something she realized Johnny did sometimes. "Don't hurt him."

Ellie had to strain to hear him. "Excuse me?" Johnny, the tough FBI agent, hardly seemed like a man who could be hurt, by her at least.

Buddy straightened and squared his shoulders. "Johnny hasn't had a lot of people he could trust in his life, including me. His grandmother and I let him down when he needed us most.".

Ellie folded her hands in front of her to avoid fidgeting, which she tended to do when she was nervous.

"Did he tell you his mother died of a drug overdose when he was twelve?"

Sadness, empathy, regret swept over her. She indicated yes with a slight tilt of her head.

"His grandmother had never forgiven our daughter for getting into drugs and she took that out on Johnny by extension." He shook his head. The overhead kitchen lights caught the glimmer of unshed tears. "It was wrong, but some people can't see past their hurt."

"I'm sorry."

Buddy nodded. "Me, too."

Duke hung by his master's side as if he sensed his sadness. His bowl of food sat untouched.

"I'm not one to speak, but if you can, don't hurt Johnny. He could use something good in his life. Something like you." The old man smiled, but the sadness in his eyes tore at her heart. "I see the way he looks at you."

Something unexplainable coiled around her heart. Johnny had a way of looking at her? She glanced down, feeling a warm blush heat her face. Hadn't she seen it herself? It was more than just a stolen kiss.

Johnny really did care about her.

She wanted to tell Buddy she had no intentions of leading Johnny on, or of getting involved in a serious relationship, that her focus was on being independent, not relying on anyone. She had been burned before.

But so had Johnny. Her heart broke for the twelve-year-old boy who had lost his mother to drugs and an overwhelming sadness swept over her. No wonder the man was relentless in his pursuit of drug dealers. It was more than a job for him. She had no idea what the future held for her and Johnny, but she had no plans to hurt him.

"I'll do my best." Ellie squeaked the words out.

"That's all that any of us can do." Buddy patted Duke's head and smiled at Ellie. "That's all we can do."

Johnny decided to run by Tony's house after learning he wasn't at the bakery. Johnny parked on the street in front of Tony's modest ranch-style home on the outskirts of Williamstown. He stepped out of the car and scanned the neighborhood. He had seen many well-kept neighborhoods where people took pride in their lawns and flowerbeds, but neither seemed to be the case here. Off in the distance, a dog barked.

Johnny strode up to the front stoop. Crickets chirped. He swatted at a mosquito buzzing around his face. The sense someone was watching him made his scalp prickle. He glanced over his shoulder, but couldn't see beyond the dim light flowing out from the house.

He extended his arm to ring the bell when the door flew open. He expected to see Tony and was surprised to find Ashley standing in the doorway.

Concern flashed in her eyes, but her mouth held a curious smile. "Special Agent Johnny Rock, to what do I owe the pleasure?"

"Hello, Ashley." Johnny looked past her and down a narrow hall. "Tony home?"

The forced smile slipped from Ashley's face. "No, I was hoping he was. We were supposed to go to the movies tonight. He hasn't been answering his cell phone, so I came over and let myself in. Sometimes he crashes in front of the TV and doesn't hear a thing. But he's not here." She shrugged. "We've been dating awhile and I have a key." She held it up, as if to prove to him she did, indeed, have a key.

"Mind if I come in and look around?" He held the screen door open with his shoulder.

Ashley angled her head and narrowed her eyes. "I told you he's not here. Why would you want to look around?"

"Something came up and I need to talk to Tony." Johnny was purposely vague. Ashley was a chatterbox and even though she knew about the investigation, Johnny didn't want her to know they were focusing on Tony.

She pressed her hand to her chest and batted her blue eyes. This young woman was an experienced flirt, far different than her best friend, Ellie. What had kept these women friends after all these years?

"Is my Tony in trouble?"

Johnny made a noncommittal sound. "I need to talk to him."

Ashley flung her hair over her shoulder and shrugged. "I wish I knew where he was myself." A brisk breeze ruffled her hair. "Oh, come in. I'm cold," she said, raising her shoulders in an exaggerated shudder.

Without waiting to be escorted beyond the front hall, Johnny strode toward the kitchen and scanned the countertops. The place was free of clutter, hardly looked lived in, and seemed too neat for a single guy.

Apparently reading his expression Ashley said, "I hired a cleaning lady for this place when we started dating." She screwed up her face. "I couldn't stand coming over here with his piles of stuff and carpets that hadn't been vacuumed in forever. It was kinda gross." Ashley winced and shook her head slightly. "I have *no* idea where he is tonight."

She reached into her oversize purse sitting on the kitchen table. She pulled out her cell phone and Johnny worried that she'd reach Tony before he did. "Don't tell him I'm looking for him."

Ashley stopped and planted a fisted hand on her hip. "Tell me what's going on."

"Who does Tony hang out with, besides you?"

She dropped her arms to her sides. "I haven't known him that long. But we've been spending most of our time together. The only time we're not together is when he's working." She scrunched up her nose. "He works a lot."

"He's not at the bakery now. I checked."

"Me, too." Ashley frowned.

"What does he do when you're working and he's not?"

"Lately that hasn't been that much, right? With all the craziness that's been going on." She didn't seem too sorry.

"The gift shop really isn't your thing, is it?"

Ashley twirled a strand of hair around her finger and took a step back, resting her hip on the counter. "Not really. It's boring. I thought it would be fun, but it's…boring," she repeated, as if finding another word was too much effort. "I didn't mind investing the money initially, but I'm not really into it anymore. And the way things are going, I can't afford to keep investing in it."

"That's unfortunate." For both Ellie and Ashley.

Ashley traced a line on the worn linoleum with the toe of her chic shoe. "You know…Ellie's a lot tougher than you think."

Johnny arched an eyebrow. "I wouldn't presume otherwise."

"It's just…" Ashley dragged her hand through her long blond hair in a practiced move. "She likes to pretend she's the victim and get people to do things for her." She took a step closer to him and he stepped back.

"I don't get that vibe from her." Johnny glanced toward the front door, willing Tony to appear so he could end this awkward conversation. The last thing he wanted to do was to alienate Ashley. It was better to have as many people as he could on his side. Working to find the truth.

A niggling started at the base of his brain.

Maybe Ashley and Tony were closer than she let on. Maybe Ashley knew…

"How come you went into business with Ellie?"

Ashley spun around and waved her hand, whatever had drawn her to him now forgotten. "She needed financial backing."

"And you have money?"

She glanced back at him. Her perfectly groomed eyebrow twitched as if that were a stupid question. "My father has money." She shrugged. "He makes sure I have what I need."

The way she said it made him think money wasn't everything.

"Will your father always provide for you?"

"I thought you came here to talk to Tony. What's with the interrogation?"

Johnny smiled, trying to lighten the mood. "Just making small talk until Tony comes home."

Ashley gathered her hair up into a ponytail in jerky motions and fastened it. Then, with a hand pressed to his back, she pushed him toward the front door. "I'm sorry, Johnny. I don't think Tony's coming home anytime soon." They both stepped out onto the front porch. She locked the dead bolt with the key and dropped it into her purse.

"Call his cell phone. Maybe you'll have better luck than me."

Johnny got back into his car and watched as Ashley crossed the yard and climbed into hers. Something he said to her had obviously set her off.

He thrummed his fingers on the steering wheel. Perhaps money and her father were sensitive subjects.

Ellie sat on the cozy brown couch while Johnny's grandfather dozed in his recliner. He insisted she call him Buddy. The notion made her smile.

She turned her phone over in her hand, itching to receive news from Johnny. She resisted the urge to call him, fearing she'd interrupt him while he was questioning Tony. A book, a classic mystery, sat unopened on her lap. She wasn't sure why she'd picked a mystery, considering she had enough of that in her life right now.

Tapping her fingers on her cell phone case, she glanced over her shoulder at the expanse of windows overlooking the backyard. During the day they provided a gorgeous view of the yard and all the trees changing colors. But now? Now, all she saw was the reflection of the contents in the room, including her worried eyes.

Didn't his grandfather believe in curtains?

Ellie slouched down in the couch, trying to make herself invisible. She redirected her attention to the television, but couldn't get into an old rerun of some detective show. She didn't want to go to bed, either—not until Johnny got home.

Had Tony been dealing drugs and using her address to ship them? Then when that one package went missing, had he gone after her, thinking she'd stolen the package?

A knot tightened in her stomach. Was Ashley in trouble? Once again she checked the display on her cell phone. She couldn't call her friend, either. Not yet. Johnny would be mad if Ellie tipped Ashley off, who could, in turn, tip off her boyfriend. No, she had to be patient and wait for Johnny.

Duke's claws clacked on the floor as he moved toward the French doors. He sat and stared outside. "What's out there, Duke?" She squinted into the darkness and her knees grew weak.

Duke stood and started whining. Then it hit her.

"Oh, you need to go out."

Ellie bit her lip and glanced over her shoulder. She set her phone and the book aside and got up from the couch. Johnny's grandfather was sound asleep in the recliner, his mouth gaping open. With a hand on the handle of the French door, she was about to tell the elderly man his dog needed out, but then it seemed silly. She was right here. She could let Duke out.

Ellie had never owned a pet because her mom was allergic, but surely she could handle letting the dog out. Ellie reached down to her side and petted Duke's head. "Okay." She unlocked the door and before she pushed it open, whispered, "Don't go far."

She opened the door and a rush of cool air hit Ellie's face. Duke slipped through the gap, his tail whacking her as he passed. Ellie patted the wall, found a light switch and flipped it, washing the patio in light. Duke stopped, looked back toward her and then returned to sniffing the border of the patio before disappearing beyond the ring of light.

Maybe he needed his privacy. She smiled and

found herself humming a song she had heard on the radio while in the car with Johnny.

Standing in the doorway, she searched the yard. Where was Duke?

From the road running alongside the corner property, a car honked. The noise made Buddy snore louder and then settle back into his chair.

Ellie squinted into the darkness. "Duke," she whispered. "Come on, boy." She crossed her arms to stave off the chill winding its way up her spine.

Tapping her fingers on her arm, she looked back at the old man. With a burst of confidence, she slipped through the opening, then closed the door quietly behind her. "Duke," she called a little louder. "Where'd you go, boy?"

Maybe she wasn't supposed to let him out without a leash. No, she was sure she had seen Buddy let him run free.

She ran a hand across the back of her neck. Dread knotted her stomach. She couldn't let anything happen to the golden retriever. What if the yard wasn't fully fenced as she had assumed?

She muttered to herself, "I should have never let Duke out. Not without checking with Buddy first.

"Duke!" she called again. Her pulse thrummed loudly in her ears. Why wasn't he making any noise? Surely he'd come when he was called.

Unless he had taken advantage of her ignorance and bolted.

No, no, no, she reassured herself. Duke seemed like such a well-trained animal. Maybe he wasn't coming because she wasn't his master.

She crossed her arms tightly around her middle and moved closer to the tree line. Squinting into the darkness, she called Duke's name again.

A hand came around the back of her and covered her mouth roughly. She tried to scream, but her attacker's hand muffled the sound.

Icy adrenaline pumped through her veins. Panic made her nauseous. She lifted her foot, slammed it backward and her heel made contact with his shin. He cursed in a harsh whisper and grabbed her tighter so that her upper teeth jammed into the soft flesh of her mouth.

All the things she had learned about self-defense crashed and tumbled in her mind. She couldn't think straight and she couldn't reason with him because he had her mouth clamped shut. Then something came to her. She let all her muscles relax letting her weight fall; harder than she imagined considering her brain was screaming, "Fight, fight, fight."

Her attacker muttered again. She couldn't tell if it was Tony or not and she wasn't sure what she should reveal. He released his hand from her mouth and Ellie crumpled to the ground.

"If you scream, I'll kill you."

Planting her hands on the cool grass, Ellie swallowed hard and gulped in a huge lungful of fresh air.

Dear Lord, please save me. Please let me think straight so I can get out of this mess.

She started to lift her head when the man hooked an arm around her neck and dragged her into the cluster of trees.

"Why are you doing this?" she asked, her voice raspy.

"You have something I want."

She tried to shake her head, but only managed to have him tighten his hold around her neck. "I don't have your package."

"I'm done playing this game. You return what's mine and I'll leave you alone."

"I don't have anything." Frustration and fear laced her voice.

"If you don't care about your own worthless life, maybe you care about your family. Your friends…" He seemed to be trying to disguise his voice. "Your friend's dog."

A wave of confidence swept over her. "Tony, is that you?" She craned her neck to see, but the man tightened his hold. "I don't have your package."

A mirthless laugh bubbled up from his throat.

"You want to play it this way?" He growled, making the fine hairs on her arms shiver.

"I'm not playing it *any* way. I don't know what you're talking about."

The muffled sound of a dog barking seemed to attract her attacker's attention. "Bring the package to the bakery. I'm done fooling around." He slipped his hand from around her neck and, planting both hands on her back, shoved her hard.

Ellie flew forward and landed hard, thankfully catching herself with her hands. She spun around to face him, ready to fend the man off in her vulnerable position seated on the ground. But no one was there. She strained to see into the shadows of the trees but only caught the sounds of leaves crunching underfoot.

She stood and glanced toward the safety of the house, then toward the sound of Duke's barking.

Her eyes scanned the yard. She noticed a metal garden tool on a small table next to the door. She ran over and picked it up, feeling the weight of it in her shaky hand. She examined its pointy tip and a sick feeling rolled through her.

Holding it tightly, she marched toward the sound of Duke's now-whimpering cries.

ELEVEN

Johnny slowed when he turned onto Treehaven. No matter how many times he came home to his grandfather's house, he got an empty feeling in the pit of his stomach. Maybe it was because his grandparents had first denied him a home when his mother—their daughter—had died. Or maybe it was because his mother had grown up here. She had existed as a person before she became his mother. Before she became addicted to drugs.

How different all their lives would have been if she had made different choices in her life.

Johnny stopped at the cross street running alongside his grandfather's house. The dome light on a small sedan caught his attention. He waited at the stop sign as the man helped a dog out of the backseat. Duke?

Johnny's adrenaline spiked. He turned and slowed next to the car. The man grabbed the dog's collar and glanced up at him, revealing his face under the lamppost.

"Tony?" Johnny muttered. The man looked as though he wanted to run.

Johnny jammed his car into Park and jumped out. He intercepted Tony as he tried to take off down the street. On the sidewalk, Duke barked frantically as if to say, "Go get 'im."

Johnny watched as Tony stopped and seemed to study the thick crop of trees lining his grandfather's property.

Johnny didn't hold on to Tony, but he was ready to grab him if he tried to make a run for it.

"Hush, Duke." The dog was in a frenzy that sent Johnny's nerves buzzing.

"What's going on here, Tony?"

"Um… I…" He looked away. "I was driving down the street and I noticed this dog out wandering. I thought I'd pull over to see if I could find its owner."

"I saw you pulling him out of your car."

Tony's eyes widened. "No." He laughed—a nervous sound. "I was trying to get him into the car."

Johnny studied the man carefully. He knew how to read people and Tony was lying and afraid. His patience dwindling, Johnny said, "Tell me the truth. What's going on?"

Tony rubbed the back of his neck and glanced toward the tree line again. He opened his mouth to say something, then clamped it shut. He pounded a fist on the lid of his trunk and cursed. "You have no idea."

Johnny thought about what Kerry had told him. The man with the orange-and-yellow sneakers had paid him to break the windows on Ellie's shop. "Maybe I do."

Tony's eyes flared wide before he seemed to catch himself. "I don't have any idea what you're talking about."

Johnny towered over Tony. "Stop with the lies."

Tony clamped his mouth closed and shook his head. "I just stopped to help the dog. That's all. This is your dog?"

"You know it's my grandfather's dog." Johnny patted Duke's head to settle him down. He whimpered, but still seemed ready to pounce at something.

"No good deed goes unpunished, huh?" Tony tried to make light of the situation.

A rustling in the trees caught their attention. Duke barked frantically, but didn't advance past the sidewalk. He'd always made a better alarm system than actual guard dog.

Johnny's heart sank when Ellie burst through the trees, a sharp garden tool in her hands and a crazed look in her eyes. "He…" She struggled to catch her breath. "…he attacked me."

Tony took a step, as if to bolt, when Johnny slammed him hard against the car. Tony grunted, but didn't say anything. Johnny snapped on handcuffs and spun him around, allowing him to rest his backside against the vehicle.

"Are you okay?" Johnny cupped her cheek. He ran his thumb across her smooth flesh, brushing off a spot of dirt.

Ellie nodded. "It *was* him," she said, pointing a shaking finger at his colorful sneakers. "He thinks I have one of his packages."

A look of defeat crossed Tony's face.

"Did you attack Ellie?"

Tony hiked his chin in a defiant gesture, but he didn't answer.

"He did. He did." Ellie was frantic. "I let Duke out and when Duke didn't return—" she wiped at her cheek "—I had to make sure Duke was okay. Then Tony grabbed me from behind."

"That's why you had Duke in your car. You wanted to lure Ellie out of the house when he didn't return."

"How did he know I was here?" Ellie smoothed a hand over her hair.

"He was probably watching the house. Knew I was gone and waited for an opportunity. Your letting out Duke was his chance." Johnny stepped closer to Tony. "What would you have done if she hadn't come outside? Break in? Knock on the door?"

A steely look crossed Tony's eyes as he leaned

in close, not taking kindly to being threatened. "You can't prove anything."

"We have a witness."

Tony's eyes grew wide.

"Kerry Pitz is awake and talking."

Ellie sat on the steps just inside the front door of the old Victorian. Buddy, who had slept through the excitement, was making her tea.

Ellie had a clear view through the sidelight windows of Officer Bailey's cruiser parked on the street where Johnny and the officer stood talking. The burly man had listened to her version of events and had promptly taken Tony into custody. But once she'd started shivering, Johnny had encouraged her to go inside. She threaded and unthreaded her fingers, unable to dispel the hum of energy buzzing through her.

Were her troubles over? Was this it? With Tony in custody, could she go about her business? But if she didn't have the package of drugs, who did?

The taillights on the cruiser glowed red and Ellie curled her fingers around the lip of the step. She crossed and uncrossed her legs until Johnny *finally* walked through the front door. He stopped abruptly and widened his eyes in surprise when he found her sitting on the steps. The concern on his face almost made her burst into tears, but she didn't want to be weak. She had been working for months now to become independent and had almost lost everything because of this Tony jerk.

Absentmindedly, she touched her mouth, remembering how Tony's coarse hand had pressed her lips tight against her teeth. Something about the encounter niggled at the far reaches of her brain, but she wasn't willing to explore that right now.

"Are you okay?" The intensity on Johnny's face unnerved her. He grabbed the newel post and lowered himself next to her, his thigh brushing hers.

His presence made her feel safe, protected. "I'm okay now that you're here."

So much for Miss Independence, her internal voice mocked.

"Can I get you some tea, too, Johnny?" Buddy called from the kitchen.

"Sounds good. We'll come back to the kitchen in a minute."

Johnny bumped shoulders with Ellie and patted her knee. "I wish I had come home sooner so Tony wouldn't have had the chance to attack you."

"If it wasn't tonight, it would have been eventually. He was waiting and watching for an opportunity. Pretty stupid that I gave him one."

"Duke needed to be let out. Don't be hard on yourself. Your heart was in the right place." He ran a hand across his chin. "I like that you were worried about Duke. It shows what kind of person you are."

Tenderness spread through her heart. "I'd never want anything to happen to Duke…" She replayed the scenario in her head and winced when she remembered Tony's threats. She looked up. "We got him. We finally got him."

Johnny nodded, but something dark flitted in the depths of his eyes.

"Don't you believe Tony's guilty? Did he admit to breaking into my apartment?"

Johnny leaned his elbows on the stair behind him. "Tony's pretty tight-lipped right now. But he's most definitely guilty of something. I'll feel better when I have a few more pieces of the puzzle in place. See if anyone else is involved."

"Maybe after he spends some time in prison he'll open up."

"Yeah," Johnny said noncommittally. "I'll talk to him tomorrow. Let him stew a bit."

Ellie's cell phone rang and she ignored it. "I bet it's Ashley." She shook her head. "I dread talking to her."

"Maybe she can get Tony to open up," Johnny said.

"I don't know. For my whole life, Ashley has been very loyal to *all* her friends. I doubt she'd say anything against Tony." Ellie shifted to rest her back against the curved wall hugging the staircase.

"Do you think she had anything to do with the package of drugs sent to your shop?"

She shook her head; the energetic back-and-forth making her brain hurt. "No, no way. I'd know." Her mind flashed back to her brother's recent acknowledgment that he *had* sold drugs. His high-paid lawyer, not his innocence, had spared him a prison sentence.

A fate Roger Petersen hadn't been spared.

"What about Roger? Maybe Tony was working with Roger?"

"I asked Tony if he had any ties to Roger, but he claims he hardly knows the guy. I'm afraid we're going to have to wait until Tony decides to open up. Or until we find concrete evidence."

Johnny pushed a hand through his hair, leaving thick tufts standing on end. She tucked her hands under her thighs to spare herself the embarrassment of reaching out and smoothing them. He caught her eye and an amused twinkle lit his eyes, as if he was reading her mind.

Then a sober expression swept over his features. "I don't know what I would have done if something had happened to you."

Heat warmed her cheeks. "I'm okay." Ellie pushed off the stairs and stood. "Do you think it's safe for me to go home?"

If she hadn't been watching his face, she might have missed the look of disappointment that flickered across his features.

"Is that what you want?"

She held up her hands and shrugged. "I'd hate to inconvenience you and your grandfather longer than necessary."

"You're no inconvenience."

Ellie turned to see Johnny's grandfather in the doorway. He was a thinner, older, grayer version of Johnny. "Tea's getting cold."

Johnny stood. "Thank you."

He guided Ellie to the kitchen with a hand on the small of her back.

"Looks like Johnny caught the bad guy," Ellie said to Buddy.

"Is that true?" Buddy asked, jerking his head back in a shaky motion.

"Yes. I still have some wrap-up to do, but looks like we have our guy."

"Does this mean you'll be headed back to Buffalo?"

Ellie's stomach dropped and she stuffed her hands into her jeans' pockets, pulling her arms tight against her sides. She hoped this was the look of a woman who didn't care, but she feared she wasn't a very good actress.

"We still have some loose ends, including the missing package. I hate to think it'll never be found…" Johnny muttered something indiscernible. "I won't be running back to Buffalo right away."

"Good," Buddy said, seemingly satisfied, "maybe I do want you to help me get this place up to snuff. Let some young family come in and fill it with kids. Give the place some new life."

Johnny smiled and his eyes brightened, as if surprised. "I'd be happy to help, Grandpa."

His grandfather's eyes drifted to Ellie. "Well, when you're not busy helping Ellie. I think she might need your help getting her gift shop re-opened. I mean, since you have time." Half his mouth crooked into a lopsided grin. He looked so much like his grandson. "Then, you can help me. I've been here for nearly sixty years. A little more time won't hurt."

"What about making way for that family?" Johnny laughed.

"Who says I'm not?"

Ellie didn't dare turn to look at Johnny, feeling his warm gaze on the side of her face.

The next morning, Ellie dusted the shelves of her neglected little gift shop. She couldn't shake a pervasive sense of loss, perhaps due to current events or maybe because she feared her business venture would never blossom.

It's autumn, she reminded herself. Then Christmas. Surely the residents of Williamstown would welcome the opportunity to buy some unique gifts from her little shop for Christmas.

"Unless they buy online," she muttered to herself.

She had remained at Johnny's grandfather's house since Johnny felt there were still some loose ends. It didn't take much to convince her because a part of her wasn't ready to be alone, save for the few hours in her shop during the day. They hoped Tony's arrest had put a damper on anyone's plans to harass Ellie, *if* there was anyone else involved. To be safe, Johnny promised to stop by and to request increased police patrols on Main Street. Johnny also promised he'd go with her to her apartment later today to help her clean up from the break-in.

Ellie tossed aside her dust rag to open a music box and listen to the soft chimes. Sadness bit at the back of her nose. Nothing had gone as she had dreamed.

Ellie took a deep breath, surprised to smell the familiar baked goods next door. She had expected it to be closed, but then again, Bobby Vino, Tony's father, came from another generation where the work ethic was strong. And memories were stronger. Her stomach hollowed out. She'd have to face the elder Vino eventually, but not right now.

She closed the music box and set it on the glass shelf.

One day at a time.

The bells on the door clacked and she was about to say, "We're not open, yet," when she noticed the smooth sheen of Ashley's hair. Ellie's heart sank. She had left three messages for Ashley, but her best friend since kindergarten had ignored each one. By the strained look on Ashley's face, Ellie knew the news of Tony's arrest hadn't escaped her.

Ellie opened her mouth, but couldn't find the words.

Ashley stopped in front of the counter, eyes protruding in accusation. Ellie had seen that look many times before, but it had never been directed at her.

"I'm sorry," Ellie finally said. Not sorry that Tony had been arrested, just sorry that someone Ashley trusted had turned out to be untrustworthy.

Sadly, Ellie knew the feeling.

"No, you're not." Ashley's skin fired red. "You're not happy unless everyone is as miserable as you are."

Ellie took a step back and banged the heel of her shoe on the wall. "I...I..."

"I...I..." Ashley mocked her. "You know as well as I do that Tony would never be involved with dealing drugs." She held her palm up to the wall separating their shop from the bakery next door. "He's a successful businessman."

Ellie gripped the edges of the counter to steady herself. "That's not entirely true."

Ashley angled her head, as if daring Ellie to press on. Ellie was not going to let her friend intimidate her.

"Tony told me that his father had hoped to expand into this—"

"They wouldn't expand the bakery if they were struggling!" Ashley must have believed a high-decibel argument was more convincing.

Ellie held her ground. "They couldn't get the loan."

"Is that what that two-faced FBI boyfriend of yours told you? He's wrong. Just like he was wrong about your brother."

Ellie resisted the instinct to lash out at her friend. Ashley seemed to be deflating with each word. How could Ellie tell her that Johnny was right about her brother? In a way, Ellie felt as though she would be telling a story that was only her brother's to tell. That she'd be betraying him.

"Some things are not as they seem." Ellie swallowed hard, carefully crafting her words. "I would never intentionally hurt you. Or anyone." How could her friend think the worst of her? A sinking feeling settled in her gut. Was she that bad at judging people's character? Ellie hiked up her chin. "We're going to have to let the legal system work it out."

Ashley tossed her hair over her shoulder. "I'm not sure I can be in business with someone who doesn't trust my judgment. I'm telling you, Tony would never deal drugs. *Never.*" Her lip began to quiver and Ellie wanted to reach out and pull her friend into an embrace, but knew it wouldn't be well received.

"Please, Ashley," Ellie said calmly, stepping out from behind the counter, "don't do anything rash." She held out her hands, palms down. "Just let the dust settle."

But hadn't Ellie known this was coming all along?

Ashley slowly shook her head. "You're not a very good friend." She spun around, her golden locks flying as she marched to the front door. "And don't expect me to work any shifts. I'm going to meet with my lawyer to see how I can get this business relationship dissolved."

Ellie watched the door long after her so-called friend stormed out in dramatic fashion. The slow burn of anger seared her gut. Ashley had a way of making everything about her. And now she had effectively told Ellie she wasn't going to be in business with her anymore.

Ellie pounded her fist on the counter, then immediately regretted it. She was caught between a rock and a hard place. Ellie needed Ashley's start-up money to make a go of the shop.

So much for independence.

Had she ever really had it?

"Having a rough day?" Johnny's words mingled with the clatter of the bells on the door. He had obviously seen Ashley storm out.

"I take it she's not happy about her boyfriend."

Ellie shook her head. "You'd think I made him sell drugs."

Johnny scratched his head. "I need to talk to Tony's father, but I wanted to check in on you first."

"I'm fine. I'm hoping it's not another quiet day here." She felt as if she was attempting to crawl up a down escalator. "I should bring in my paints and easel. At least then I could do something productive while I waited for customers."

The compassion in Johnny's eyes made her heart melt.

"I wanted to tell you something…" His voice trailed off as something seemed to catch his attention. "Hold on, Mr. Vino's headed this way."

A short man in a white baker's coat yanked open the front door and stepped into the shop. He seemed to come up short when he noticed Johnny standing there.

Ellie stepped forward, feeling a bit more confident with Johnny here. "Hello, Mr. Vino. I'm sorry about Tony. Are you doing okay?"

Mr. Vino pulled a handkerchief out of his pocket and mopped his forehead. "I don't know if my Tony did all these things, but if he did, he did them for me."

Ellie flinched, startled at his contrite tone. She had been bracing for another tongue-lashing.

"I've done nothing but worry about this shop. About money. About how we're going to close if business didn't turn around. If…" The husky man swallowed hard. "If Tony was selling drugs, he was doing it to help with the bakery. To get some creditors off my back." The worry in his eyes broke Ellie's heart.

"Did you know about his activities?" Johnny asked.

Mr. Vino shook his head vigorously. "No. No."

Johnny placed a hand on the man's shoulder. "Whatever Tony's reason, a high school student overdosed on drugs. It's not a game…or a get-rich-quick scheme."

Mr. Vino's eyebrows pulled together, forming an exclamation over the point of his bulbous nose. "Do you have evidence he was selling the drugs?"

"Tony confessed this morning." Johnny shifted to look at Ellie. Apparently a night in lockup did the trick. "That's what I wanted to tell you."

Mr. Vino's forehead creased. "He confessed?"

"Yes, sir. I'm sorry." Johnny touched the man's sleeve. All the color seemed to drain from Mr. Vino's face. "Is there someone I can call for you?"

The baker snatched the hat from his head. "No, no…" He looked up with hope in his glistening eyes. "I'm going to see that he has the best lawyer." He shook his head. "I raised him better."

Ellie's stomach hurt. She flashed back to her own parents' heartbroken expressions when her brother had been arrested. How they had insisted on—and believed in—the innocence of their Golden Boy.

Any words of comfort got lodged in Ellie's throat.

"Mr. Vino, what can I do for you?" Johnny asked again.

Mr. Vino raised his hand and dropped it in disgust. "Nothing." He turned and slowly walked out of the shop.

Ellie planted her palms on the counter for support. "We gave you a lot of grief when my brother was arrested."

Johnny stuffed his hands into the front pockets of his jeans. "It comes with the territory. Truth be told, we never arrest a guilty person." He quirked an eyebrow and she detected a glint of amusement in his eyes.

"Then I guess it's a good thing Tony confessed."

Johnny grimaced slightly. "It seemed too easy."

Ellie tilted her head, waiting for him to go on.

"He seemed afraid." He ran the palm of his hand across his jaw. "Of what, I'm not sure. He confessed to everything, including shipping drugs to your address and the break-in. He claims he lost track of one package and thought you stole it."

Knees weak, Ellie lowered herself onto the stool she kept behind the counter. "And he really thinks *I* stole it?"

Johnny nodded.

"I didn't."

"I know. I'll have to track it down."

"What if you never find it?" Ellie felt lightheaded. "Will anyone else be looking for it? Usually there's a chain of drug dealers involved, right?"

"Yes, but Tony claims he never told anyone he suspected you had it. He claims he was trying to scare you into returning it. If he's telling me the truth, your harassment stops with Tony Vino's arrest."

Ellie bit her lower lip. What if Tony was lying?

TWELVE

The wild wind tossed a dried leaf against the window at the end of the upstairs hallway of the old Victorian. Johnny pulled back the lacy curtain and squinted at the dark rain cloud in an otherwise blue sky. The late-afternoon sunlight accentuated the ominous silver quality of the cloud. The gold and red leaves against the steel-gray rain cloud made him think of Ellie. He could imagine her scrunching up her nose and touching her mouth with the back of a paintbrush, giving it careful consideration before she touched brush to canvas.

She had a keen eye and a talent that he sensed she didn't appreciate. No, a talent she didn't have faith in.

He hoped the rain held off for the church carnival later this afternoon. He had seen first-hand how hard the youth had worked on getting ready for the big fund-raiser. It would be a shame if rain kept people away.

Johnny checked the time on his cell phone, then shoved it into his back pocket.

No more stalling.

He swallowed hard and turned to the closed door at the end of the hall. His mother's childhood bedroom. He had promised his grandfather he'd pack up her things because his grandfather couldn't. Now that the case was mostly wrapped up, he had the time.

He reached out and clutched the glass doorknob. Inwardly, he chuckled. He had faced down the worst of the worst, people who'd sooner shoot you than say hello. But the thought of entering his mother's room made his lungs ache.

He turned the handle and the hinges groaned, protesting years of disuse. He wondered how long the room had been closed. Had his grandparents thought shutting the door could shut out the memories of their only daughter?

He stepped into the large bedroom. Dust motes danced in the thin slivers of sunlight slipping in around the drawn blinds. The musty smell reached his nose and he held back a sneeze.

Johnny stood in one spot and took in the room. The peach-colored bedspread covered the bed. A stuffed kitten sat among the pillows. Tingles bit the back of his nose. He had a hard time imagining his mother as a kid. A happy kid.

He bit the side of his cheek and walked over

to her dresser. The floor creaked under his footsteps. Lying flat on the white dresser was a dust-covered photo. His vision narrowed. It was his mother…and him. With a shaky hand, he picked up the photo and ran his finger over her face and his.

"She really loved you."

Johnny spun around. His grandfather stood in the doorway, bracing himself on the doorjamb.

He shuffled into the bedroom, his eyes roaming the space as if he had forgotten what it looked like.

"Your mom came back with you when you were about three years old." His grandfather took the photo from Johnny's hands and stared at it. "She told me she was determined to get clean. To do right by you."

Johnny lowered himself to sit on the edge of the bed. It creaked under his weight. "How long did she stay?"

"For about a year."

Johnny ran his hand along the stitching on the bedspread. "I didn't know."

Buddy set the photo on the dresser and patted it, as if he were patting the head of the small child in the photo. He slowly turned around. "Your grandmother was so excited to get you enrolled in the church preschool program."

Johnny stared at his grandfather, his words

ping-ponging around his brain. He had lived here? For a year in his young life? No wonder so many things seemed vaguely familiar; he'd thought maybe his mother's description had gotten into his head. His mother had only said horrible things about her parents…this place. But he had realized his mother's description had been skewed when he'd finally gotten to know his grandfather.

"Your grandmother's heart was broken when Mary Claire packed you up and left."

Johnny's chest grew heavy. "Why did she leave? I can't imagine she could afford a roof over her head and food. Not as nice as this."

"That's what her mother and I thought." He wrapped his fingers into a fist and tapped on the footboard. "We couldn't convince her otherwise."

Johnny ran a hand across his chin. "She had a new boyfriend."

His grandfather didn't answer, but his expression said it all. *How did you know?*

"All my mother's big decisions revolved around men. Men and drugs."

"I never understood what her mother and I did wrong."

A realization crept into Johnny's soul and filled his heart. "God gave us all free will." He let out a heavy sigh. "My mother made her own choices." Even Johnny couldn't sway his mother's heart. A new love—or what she thought was love—and drugs were far more powerful than a little kid.

And it wasn't his fault.

Buddy's strong hand cupped Johnny's shoulder. "Don't let your mom's mistakes ruin your life."

Johnny looked up and tilted his head, confused.

"You got the guy who was dealing drugs. You did a good thing. But there has to be more to life than chasing bad guys."

"Tony Vino is still adamant he was working alone. But something about this case bugs me."

"Are you sure you're not focusing on the case to avoid your personal life?"

Johnny studied the pink, purple and yellow flowered area rug. "I like chasing bad guys."

"It's something you can control."

"To a degree."

"There's more to life than work."

Johnny scratched his head, waiting for his grandfather to continue.

"Your mother left you. Then your grandmother and I let you down when you needed us. We were blinded by our own hurt."

Johnny patted the bed and stood. He turned to face his grandfather. "You were hurting. I understand."

Buddy shook his head, the lines around his mouth growing deeper. "You've surrounded yourself with work because you don't want to get hurt again."

Johnny bit back a smirk. "I'm not into this touchy-feely stuff, Gramps. I work hard because we arrest one drug dealer and there's another one right behind him."

"You can still catch the bad guys, but why not take time to enjoy your life? That Ellie girl is very sweet."

Johnny laughed, but the memory of her soft lips sobered him. "Ellie's not much into relationships, either." How many times had she let him know she wanted to be independent? That she'd been burned before by a longtime boyfriend.

"The two of you are so caught up in your past hurts, you can't enjoy the moment." Buddy shrugged. "You're the smart FBI guy. I suppose you know best." A twinkle lit his grandfather's eyes. He lifted his hand. "Will you get me some of that apple cider they sell at the church carnival?"

Johnny smiled, knowing exactly what his grandfather had up his sleeve. "You want me to drive you down to the carnival?"

His grandfather jutted out his lower lip. "Nah, I'm tired. But if you're not going, I understand."

They both knew he'd run the errand for his grandfather. "I'd be happy to run down to the carnival. How about a candied apple while I'm there?"

His grandfather waved him away. "Not good for my teeth. But, oh…I can already taste the cider."

A stiff breeze whipped across the church parking lot. Ellie zipped up her fleece jacket and tucked her chin into the warm collar. She had been manning the cider booth for the church's youth group so they could enjoy the carnival for a while. She was happy for the distraction.

A distraction from Tony's drug arrest.

A distraction from the lack of sales at Gifts and More.

A distraction from the big question: Where was she headed in life?

If things continued, she'd have to close the shop. For good.

Stop.

Tonight was a night to relax and enjoy the moment. She loved this time of year. She closed her eyes briefly and smelled the crisp night air mixed with fried dough and apple pie. The musical notes from the main stage competed with the laughter of the families enjoying a night out.

She leaned her hip on the edge of the booth. The placard mounted at the corner of the booth read: All Proceeds For Kids Escaping Drugs.

That decision had been entirely the youths'. In past years, the funds had gone to cover social events for the kids but this year they had unanimously voted to raise money for a program to help kids who suffered from alcohol or drug dependence.

"I'll have two jugs of cider."

Ellie spun around at Johnny's voice and tried to ignore the warmth that flooded her heart. "I didn't know you were going to come tonight. I thought you'd be helping your grandfather before getting ready to return to Buffalo." Ellie crossed her arms and rolled up on the balls of her feet. For some reason she felt uncomfortable; perhaps it was the way his warm brown eyes seemed to look right into her soul.

"My grandfather told me I had to come. Told me I had to pick up some apple cider." He wrapped his hands around the handles of two jugs.

"Best cider in town." Ellie found herself smiling.

"Is there a lot of cider competition in town?" His teasing tone elicited an even bigger smile out of her.

"So…are you just grabbing the cider and leaving?"

Kaylee jogged up, a big smile on her face. "Agent Rock, you and Miss Ellie should do the maze. It's awesome. I went through it with Amy and Kendal." The two young women Ellie had met earlier trailed Kaylee.

Ellie smiled at Kaylee. She was hanging out with her friends and taking a break from the drama of boys, especially boys who had made some very bad choices lately. Last Ellie had heard, Collin Parker was out on bail awaiting arraignment.

Stupid decisions. Lifelong consequences.

"Oh, I don't know. Agent Rock has to take the cider home to his grandfather."

Kaylee dragged the cider by the lids toward her. "I can hold on to the cider until you guys get back." She checked the time on her cell phone. "It's our turn to work the booth, anyway." She flicked her fingers playfully. "Go, go, go…"

Ellie angled her head. "Really, Kaylee. You can't tell us to run along like one of your friends." She laughed as she removed her money bib and helped Kaylee tie it around her waist.

Ellie stepped outside the booth and zipped her jacket up higher. "Maybe it's time I called it a night."

Johnny gently took Ellie's elbow. "I think Miss Kaylee has a great idea." His warm breath whispered across her ear.

Ellie looked up at him with wide eyes, not sure what to think about how she felt. She had been mentally preparing herself to say goodbye to Johnny now that the investigation was wrapping up.

"I…um…" Ellie sputtered as the young woman watched her carefully. "Sure, I suppose a quick tour of the maze can't hurt."

"I'll be back shortly to get my cider," Johnny said to Kaylee.

"No problem, Agent Rock." Kaylee set the cider down behind the counter, a mischievous grin on her face.

Ah, to be young, Ellie mused.

Johnny squeezed Ellie's hand. "You okay?"

"Yeah, I was just thinking about how these young kids don't realize how many opportunities they have in front of them. What's the expression? The world is their oyster?"

Johnny winced.

"Not a fan of oysters, huh? How about, 'Youth is wasted on the young'?"

"I know what you mean. I see so many young people making bad choices. It kills me."

"Then why do you do it?" She kicked at the loose hay on the blacktop. "It must wear on you."

"It does. But someone has to do it." There was a rapt quality to his voice.

A couple smiled and waved at Johnny. Then an older man from the church came up and shook his hand. "You did a good thing, Agent Rock. Thank you."

"Does that always happen after you make an arrest?" She smiled up at him.

"No. I think it's the small-town thing going on."

"The news is touting you as hometown hero."

Johnny ran a hand through his hair. "I prefer to work under the radar."

Ellie playfully rested her cheek against his shoulder and kept walking. "When do you head back to Buffalo?"

"I took a week's vacation so I can spend more time with my grandfather. He's not quite ready to move, but we have to make a plan to assure he can continue living at the house. There's a few projects…" He shrugged. "You know how it is."

"Yeah." She tried to hide the disappointment from her voice. The wind kicked up and Ellie struggled to stifle a shudder.

Johnny let go of her hand and wrapped a hand around her shoulder. "Cold?"

Not exactly at this moment.

The clean scent of him filled her senses. This man, without saying a word, destroyed every argument she had made for herself to avoid reentering the dating world.

If only he lived in Williamstown.

Johnny stepped away from her toward another refreshment booth. "Want some hot chocolate?"

"Sure." Ellie stuffed her hands into her pockets, missing the warmth of his presence.

He paid for two hot chocolates and handed her one. "Ready for the maze?"

"I have no sense of direction."

"It's okay, I'll stay with you."

Ellie smiled, feeling like one of those young girls she envied. Feeling as if a world of opportunities stretched at her feet.

The smell of dried hay reached her nose as Johnny handed the attendant their tickets and they entered the maze made of hay bales stacked seven feet high.

A young girl ran past them at a cross section, giggling. She was obviously lost.

Johnny walked slowly, kicking at the hay. "Can't say I've ever been in a maze made of hay bales."

"Really?"

"Really."

Ellie didn't press. From what Johnny had told her, he hadn't had an idyllic childhood filled with church carnivals, hot chocolate and mazes.

"I'm not one for confined spaces," Ellie said, "but I figure I can bust out of here by knocking over the bales if necessary." She dragged her hand along the wall and pulled it back when she snagged a piece of prickly hay. The light of a passing vehicle flashed in the cracks between the bales. "See, this is the outside wall." She lifted her foot, pretending to push on the bottom bale. "One swift kick and I'm free."

"I don't think that's exactly necessary. Besides, it would ruin the fun of the maze."

"Yeah." Ellie drank the last of her hot chocolate.

Johnny held out his hand. "Let me toss that out for you. There was a garbage can near the entrance." He smirked at Ellie's raised eyebrows. "Stay right here, I'll be back in a second. I promise I won't let you get lost."

Ellie clutched her hands together and pressed them to her chest. "You'll be my hero." Besides, she had something in her shoe and could take this time to dump it out.

A slow, genuine smile crept across his face, making Ellie's insides go soft. She was in so much trouble.

Ellie rested one hand on the maze wall, careful not to push too hard, and yanked off her sneaker, tipping out the small pebble and slipping her shoe back on.

She then pulled out her cell phone and checked it, mostly out of habit. She went to put it back into her pocket when it slipped out of her hand. "Oh, man," she muttered, hoping she hadn't cracked the screen.

Just then a hay bale nudged her backside. She lost her balance and fell to her knees. Someone grabbed her arm and her first instinct was relief. "Johnny?"

The grip bit into her flesh and her relief turned to fear. She tried to yank her arm away, but the person held on tight, then wrapped another arm around her shoulder, pulling her to her feet.

The smell. Her fear. A horrible familiarity. All reminiscent of her attack while looking for Duke.

But Tony had been arrested.

Icy dread pumped through her veins.

A blood-curdling scream rent the night air. It took her a moment to realize the sound had ripped from her throat.

The man dragged her through the tumbled hay bales to an idling vehicle in the parking lot on the other side. She bucked and kicked, but he only held her tighter. As he opened the trunk, fear made her want to puke.

There, curled up in a ball, was her good friend, Ashley.

The word *Oh* barely formed on her lips when the man shoved her inside on top of Ashley.

In the brief second before the lid slammed shut, Roger Petersen's angry face came into view.

Roger?

The trunk lid slammed down, leaving her

in blackness. Terror clawed at her heart as she blinked, blinked, blinked.

Absolute darkness.

THIRTEEN

Johnny backtracked a couple turns to the entrance where he had noticed a trash can. He tossed in the two paper cups and a splash of hot chocolate landed on his hand.

"Oh, here you go, Agent Rock." An older woman hustled toward him with a couple napkins.

He smiled and took them from the woman. "Thank you."

He wiped his sticky hands and stuffed the napkins into the trash can.

"I wanted to thank you for catching the drug dealer. I can't believe it was Bobby's son." She hitched a shoulder and kept talking. "I bought my rye bread from that bakery for years." She made a tsking sound. "I suppose you never really know about anyone."

"No, ma'am." Johnny glanced toward the maze entrance, figuring Ellie would be wondering where he was.

"I heard the young boy who overdosed is doing better."

Johnny nodded.

"These kids think they're invincible." She hiked up the strap of her purse on her shoulder. "I'm glad my boys are all grown. I can't imagine handling what these kids are dealing with today. Sure, drugs have always been around, but now they have these phones and the World Wide Web. The young people today can't seem to do anything without having their photo plastered all over." She shook her head, disgusted. "I miss the simpler times."

Johnny reached out and touched her arm. "Enjoy your evening, ma'am. I have someone waiting for me."

The older lady waved her hand. "Oh, listen to me going on and on. Have a good night, Agent Rock."

"Thank you. You, too."

Johnny turned and strode back toward the maze. When he reached the entrance he heard a scream.

"Ellie!"

His heartbeat jackhammered in his chest. Breaking into a run, he made the few turns to where he had left Ellie. The wall of hay bales had collapsed. He stepped through the opening to the parking lot on the other side of the maze.

"Ellie!" he shouted again. "Ellie!"

Johnny scanned the quiet parking lot. Adrenaline surged through his veins. No sign of Ellie.

Calmly, he pulled his cell phone out of his pocket and dialed her number. A short distance away he heard her familiar ring tone. His heart stopped. He marched toward the sound. On the ground littered with hay, the screen of a smartphone lit the darkened corner. He bent and picked it up. His name lit the screen.

Ellie's phone.

Johnny straightened and searched the area. Where was Ellie?

In the close confines of the hot trunk, something sharp dug into Ellie's side. She tried to scoot forward, but she didn't want to risk hurting Ashley. The quiet up and down of Ashley's chest assured Ellie that her friend was alive. *Thank God.*

The stale smell of old upholstery and rubber assaulted her nose. Her stomach roiled and she feared she'd throw up.

Dear Lord, please protect me. Deliver Ashley and me to safety. Keep me calm. Allow me to think. Let Johnny find us in time.

The words of her prayer were as disjointed as her thoughts.

God would understand.

Ellie closed her eyes and mentally sent out a

message to Johnny. But what could she tell him? *I'm in the trunk of a car headed to who knows where?*

Ellie tried to shove aside her feelings of despair. She had to do something. She felt around the trunk for a trunk release but couldn't find one. She feared this car was too old to be outfitted with one.

With a shaky hand, she reached out and touched what felt like Ashley's arm. She gently shook her friend. "Ashley," she said in a hushed whisper. She didn't want to give Roger an excuse to pull over and hurt her. Hurt them.

Ellie dragged her hand up her friend's arm and found her face, her mouth, the duct tape over it. She picked at a corner. "Ashley?"

No answer.

Her pulse whooshed in her ears, the steady beat amplified by the confined space. A bead of sweat trickled down her face and around to her jawline.

"Ashley, I'm going to pull the tape off your mouth. I'm going to do it fast so it doesn't hurt." She had no idea if her friend could hear her. Could process her words.

Her friend groaned softly. A surge of relief swept over Ellie. Ashley was coming around.

"Try to stay quiet, honey. I'll get this tape off your mouth."

The next muffled cry that came from her friend was strangled.

"I'll try not to hurt you."

Ellie braced herself mentally and pulled the tape from her friend's mouth in one swift, hair-removing yank. Ashley whimpered.

"What's going on?" Ellie whispered to her friend. "Do you have any idea?"

Ashley coughed and Ellie held her breath, her heartbeat ticking away the seconds as the car sped down the road.

"You have to give it back," Ashley said, her voice raw, hoarse.

"What are you talking about?"

"The package. The package! You have to give it back." Ashley's frantic tone sent Ellie's already frazzled nerves into hyperdrive.

"The package of drugs?" Every inch of Ellie's skin tingled with the buzz of adrenaline.

"You have to give it back or Roger's going to kill us."

"Kill us?"

"Me, Tony…now you."

Ellie's mind swirled; random thoughts pelted her brain. "I don't have the package."

"What did you do with it?"

"I never had it." Ellie tried to keep the anger and frustration out of her tone. It would serve no purpose now. An ache shot up her shoulder and arm when the car hit a bump. "How will Roger hurt Tony? Tony's in jail."

"No. Tony got out on bail this afternoon."

None of this made sense.

The car came to a stop and a new wave of panic rolled over her. The car door creaked open. Footsteps. The sound of a key fob chirped in the black night.

And the trunk popped open. A rush of cool air swept into the confined space. Beyond the dark shadow of Roger hovering over the open trunk, Ellie saw a million stars in the sky.

Please help me, Lord.

Roger reached into the trunk and yanked Ellie out by the arm. His fingers dug into her flesh, sending an aching pain shooting through her limb. She blinked a few times against the streetlights. The alley behind her shop came into focus.

Roger slammed the trunk lid closed on her friend and Ellie yelped, "Don't leave Ashley in there."

Roger jerked her toward the back door of Gifts and More. "I think you have bigger things to worry about than Ashley."

"I—"

"Get me the package now, or I'll kill your friend."

Ellie swallowed hard. "You can't get away with this. You didn't ten years ago. You won't now."

A boldness she didn't understand filled her. Was she being smart or stupid?

Roger grunted and shook her so hard that she was forced to look back at his vehicle. "Go on, look."

Hot anger and fear flooded her face. Roger ushered her over to the car and she peered through the window. Tony lay curled up on the backseat, his hands and ankles bound, his mouth covered with duct tape. His wide eyes and jerky movements radiated terror.

"If all this goes bad, your boyfriend will think Tony Vino snapped. He'll be the only suspect."

"Tony won't keep quiet." She had enough sense not to argue the point that Johnny was hardly her boyfriend.

Under the moonlight, she could see the corner of Roger's mouth pull into a smirk. "He won't have a choice."

The implications of his words stabbed Ellie in the heart. Pinpricks of realization rolled over her. Roger would have to kill *all* of them to get away with this if he planned to pin it on Tony, making it look as though Tony had committed murder-suicide.

Ellie fisted and unfisted her hands. Her mind raced. *What should I do? What should I do?* Should she tell Roger she didn't have the package? Would that mean instant death for all of them? Should she pretend she did and buy them all time? Time for Johnny to find them.

She lifted a finger in a hold-on-a-minute gesture.

Yes, she decided, playing along was her only hope.

"Okay," Ellie said, trying to keep her voice even. "Let me get it."

Roger pushed her toward the back door of her shop. "Good girl."

Ellie stopped at the door and dug into her pocket for the keys.

Think. Think. Think.

She spun around and her stomach pitched when she noticed Roger's intense expression. "I only have the key for the front door," she said, her voice shaky.

Roger clenched his jaw and muttered something.

He grabbed her by the arm and gestured toward the car with his chin. "They ain't going anywhere," he said, referring to his hostages. He shoved Ellie down the narrow alley between the buildings. She had to jog to keep pace and not trip over her feet. A continuous prayer ran through her head.

Dear Lord, help me...

"You better not be lying to me." Roger snarled.

When they reached Main Street, it was oddly

deserted. Just her luck, everyone was at the church carnival.

Roger pulled a gun from his waistband and leaned in close, his stale breath hot on her cheek. "If we run into anyone, you tell them you're opening the shop to show me something."

Ellie nodded, unable to force any words from her too tight throat.

"I don't think I need to remind you, your friend's life is in your hands."

Idiot was going to kill all of them anyway. Did he really think she was that stupid?

Focusing solely on what she had to do, Ellie put the key into the lock of the front door with shaky fingers.

Dear Lord, help me...

She pushed open the door and slammed the alarm pad inside.

Roger cursed and reached for her, but his fingers brushed her waist.

Ellie grabbed the top of the glass shelves with both hands and toppled them in front of the door, then spun on her heels, making her way to the storage room.

A shot rang out, whizzing by her ear. She dove for the ground, her fingers touching the side of the door frame to the storage room.

Just a few more feet.

Another shot sounded and drywall exploded over her head.

Protect me, Lord.

Ellie army-crawled into the storage room. Once inside, she pivoted and slammed the door shut.

A tear ran down her cheek. Her eyes drifted to the back door leading to the alley. Could she make it to the car to save her friend before Roger got back to the alley?

Scrambling to her feet, she fumbled in the darkness to find the handle of the door. Her shaking fingers found the knob for the dead bolt, but a horrible sense of foreboding paralyzed her.

Dear Lord, what should I do?

The whimpers of a woman sounded from somewhere close.

All of Johnny's senses were on high alert. He ran toward the woman's cries around to the side of the maze. Kaylee looked up at him from a crouched position, her wet cheeks glistening under the lampposts.

Johnny scanned the church parking lot again. Nothing but a few cars and lampposts and a man in the distance emptying the garbage totes with a wary eye on the commotion.

"Kaylee, what's wrong?" Johnny took her hand and pulled her to her feet.

"He took Ellie!"

Icy dread pumped through his veins. "Who took her? What did you see?"

Kaylee slapped at the tears running down her cheeks. "A man rammed his car into the corner of the maze and grabbed Ellie. Stuffed her in the trunk. I was so afraid. I thought he might grab me." She clawed at his arm. "You have to help her."

"What man?"

"I don't know."

"Which way did they go?" He swallowed hard, relying on his training.

Kaylee lifted a shaky hand and pointed toward the side street. The car had turned right.

"What kind of car?"

"Not a big one. A regular car. Not a truck or anything."

"Do you have a phone, Kaylee?"

She looked up at him, blinking her confusion. He wasn't sure if it was due to the situation or the stupidity of his question. Of course she had a phone. Proving his point, she reached into the pocket of her hoodie and pulled out a sparkly pink phone.

"Call 9-1-1. Tell them exactly what you told me."

"What are you going to do?"

"Find Ellie."

She stared at him and Johnny worried the poor

girl was in shock. But time was ticking for Ellie. "Do you understand? Call 9-1-1."

"Yes." Kaylee lifted her phone and pressed the screen.

Johnny ran toward his car, climbed in, his breath coming out in ragged gasps. He jammed the key into the ignition and sped out of the parking lot. He had let Ellie down, just as he'd let down his mother. He hadn't been there when they both really needed him.

It was too late for his mother, but there was still hope for Ellie. An emptiness hollowed out his chest, reminding him why he never allowed anyone in. It hurt too much when they left.

Unbidden, a prayer floated to mind.

Help me find her in time. Let me save Ellie.

At the first intersection, Johnny glanced down the cross street, then it hit him. Ellie's shop. The first place he had to check was Ellie's shop. All this trouble had begun when someone believed she'd stolen a package of drugs that had been shipped to her shop's address.

Johnny turned down the street, then onto Main Street. He slowed in front of Gifts and More and his heart dropped when he noticed the front door ajar. He slammed the gearshift into Park and jumped out.

Grabbing his gun from its holster, he trained it on the dark shadows in the shop. His shoes crunched on the broken glass inside the door as he stepped over overturned shelves.

His intense focus shifted everything into slow motion.

There had been a struggle here.

In the back of the shop he saw a shadow. He tightened his grip on his gun. Too tall and broad to be Ellie.

Johnny dove behind the counter and trained his gun on the shadow against the back wall. "Identify yourself."

Tense silence filled the small space. His worry for Ellie had made Johnny careless. He should have never stormed into the shop. He could have been shot while he'd stood in the doorway.

Johnny crept to the far side of the counter, careful to keep the barrier between him and the intruder. He waited a minute for his eyes to adjust to the darkness. Then the distinct shape of a man came into focus. The man pushed away from the wall, perhaps ready to make his escape—or come after him.

Adrenaline spiked through him.

Protect me, Lord.

The man took a step forward and Johnny dove at his legs, taking him down. The man landed with a thud and a sharp curse. Something clattered across the floor.

Johnny jumped up and straddled the man's

back. He got hold of his arms and handcuffed him, the well-practiced motion fluid even in the darkness of the shop.

Johnny jerked the man to his feet and dragged him toward the light switch on the wall. He slapped it and the glaring light illuminated the shop.

Recognition shot through Johnny.

Roger Petersen.

Roger snarled at him. "I should have shot you when I had the chance."

"Why didn't you?" Johnny's fists clenched.

"I'll probably ask myself that for the rest of my life." Roger groaned. "Too many stupid witnesses," he muttered.

"*You* were Tony's boss all along. He was too afraid to give you up."

A smirk slanted Roger's mouth and Johnny shoved him down.

"What did you do with Ellie?" Johnny asked, crouching to look Roger in the eye where he sat on the floor.

Anger sliced through Johnny. That stupid smirk again.

"Who's out there?" A woman's voice floated out from behind the storage room door. *Ellie's voice.*

Relief flooded him.

Johnny jumped up and ran to the door. "Ellie, it's Johnny. Open up. It's safe."

He heard the bolt slide and then the door opened slowly, as if she didn't trust the situation. When her eyes lit on Roger sitting handcuffed in the corner, she fell out of the storage room and into Johnny's arms.

Johnny wrapped his arms around her tightly and squeezed. "You're safe. You're safe."

FOURTEEN

Ellie reluctantly stepped out of the comfort of Johnny's embrace. Her relief was quickly replaced with a knot of panic in her gut. "We need an ambulance for Ashley and Tony. We need to get Ashley out of the trunk."

Her eyes drifted to Roger who was sitting stoically in the corner, his expression not revealing much of anything. How could someone be so cold?

"He has them in his car in the alley." Her hand slid down to Johnny's hand and she pulled him toward the alley door.

"Okay, okay." Johnny laced his fingers with hers, immediately grounding her. "The police are on the way. I'll call for an ambulance."

As if he had willed him into existence, Officer Bailey stepped into the shop, his boots crunching on the glass in the doorway. Ellie spun around, a case of déjà vu making her brain feel fuzzy.

"You've got the most exciting shop in the

neighborhood, Miss Winters." Officer Bailey took in the scene. Roger Petersen sat in the corner with his hands cuffed behind his back. "Well, lookey here, Mr. Petersen." He blew out a long breath. "I guess people don't change."

Officer Bailey emitted a soft grunt as he bent over his expanding middle, grasped the man's arm and tugged Roger to his feet. "Come on, now…"

"Once you get him into custody, send an officer into the alley," Johnny said.

Bailey raised a hand in silent agreement and ushered Roger out the front door.

When Ellie and Johnny reached the alley, an officer had already helped Tony to a seated position on the backseat while an ambulance navigated the narrow alley, lights flashing.

Ellie reached inside the car and pulled the trunk release. She ran around back and found Ashley, eyes closed, a sheen of sweat on her porcelain skin. "Ashley! Ashley!" Ellie reached in and touched her friend's cheek with the back of her hand.

Her heart dropped when Ashley didn't respond.

Without saying a word, Johnny squeezed in next to Ellie and scooped up Ashley, one arm under her legs and the other around her back. He carried her over to the ambulance. The EMTs guided Ashley onto a gurney and immediately started working on her.

Ellie watched with wide eyes. *Dear Lord, let Ashley be okay.*

"How is she?" Johnny asked the EMT.

The EMT pulled the stethoscope from his ears. "Vitals seem steady. We'll get her to the hospital to check her out."

"So, she's going to be okay?" Ellie asked, her voice high-pitched.

The EMT nodded his head in reassurance, but didn't articulate his thoughts, probably because as a health-care professional, he couldn't make promises.

All the same, Ellie breathed a little easier. *Thank You, Lord.*

When they returned to Tony, the officer had already cut off the duct tape from his feet and hands. Something akin to shame lurked in the depths of his eyes.

"You ready to talk?" Johnny asked.

An EMT hustled over to Tony, but he brushed him away. "I'm fine. Get Ashley to the hospital."

Johnny gave the EMT a subtle nod and the EMT jogged toward the ambulance.

"You ready to tell me the whole truth, Tony?" Johnny put one foot up on the bumper of the car and rested his elbow on his knee. Ellie crossed her arms in front of her, trying to stay warm.

"Can I talk to my father first?" Tony ran the back of his hand under his nose.

"Why would I let you do that?" Johnny put his foot down on the pavement and crossed his arms, flicking a look in Ellie's direction before he retrained his steely gaze on Tony.

Tony held up a shaky finger and his eyes wandered to the alley door to Ellie's shop. "You got Roger Petersen in custody?"

"Yes. The local police are taking him down to the station now."

Tony closed his eyes briefly, a look of relief easing the lines around his eyes. "If you let me talk to my dad, I'll tell you everything. I need to explain everything to my dad."

Johnny ran a hand across his hair. "Okay. Talk."

"First I want to see my dad." The plea in Tony's voice broke Ellie's heart. People make stupid, life-altering decisions all the time. Her mind flashed to her brother.

Johnny shook his head. "You're gonna have to trust me."

Tony nodded. Johnny slipped his hand around the crook of Tony's elbow and pulled him to his feet. "Let's talk in the storage room. Then I'll run you home to talk to your dad."

Tony hung his head in defeat.

Without a word, Ellie followed the two men.

She noticed how close Johnny stayed to Tony, not trusting that he wouldn't make any sudden movements.

Johnny held out an open palm to the chair in the corner. Specks of Citrus Blast paint dotted the cement floor from the attack on Ellie. Had this man attacked her?

Compassion warred with anger in her tight chest. Tony had wreaked havoc on her life.

"How did you get out on bail?" Johnny asked.

"Roger paid it. From what little I was able to gather, he made some last-minute arrangements late this afternoon. On a Saturday, even. He seems to know a lot of people. I think he convinced the court I wasn't a flight risk because of my family ties."

"You didn't find him bailing you out suspicious?"

"At first, I didn't care. I was so happy to get out of that hole. My father couldn't afford to post bail. But as soon as Roger had me in the car, I knew it was a mistake. He needed me out of jail to set his plan in motion." Tony groaned. "I stupidly thought if I confessed to everything, he'd leave me and my family alone. But Roger was never going to rest until he recovered that stupid package."

"Tell me how you got involved with Roger in the first place."

Tony ran his hands up and down the thighs of his jeans, gathering his thoughts. "My family's bakery's in trouble." He looked up, worry in eyes. "Stupidly, I thought helping Roger was going to be an easy way to raise some funds."

Johnny rested a hip on the side of the utility sink. "How did you get hooked up with Roger?"

Tony studied his feet. "It's a small town." He shrugged a shoulder. "A chance reunion led to a discussion, which led to a trial run. Roger was careful to keep himself clean so that if things went south, he'd be safe. Before I knew it, I was so deep I couldn't get out if I wanted to."

"What was your job?"

"To receive the shipment of drugs and hand them over to Roger for distribution."

"That's it?" Johnny rubbed a hand across the back of his neck.

"You used the address for my shop to ship drugs?" Ellie finally found her voice.

"I had to protect the bakery."

Ellie shook her head. "What if I had opened the package? What if I had gotten to it first?"

"I was tracking the packages. I knew exactly when they were supposed to arrive so I could intercept them."

"How? Didn't the delivery driver question you?" Ellie asked, growing agitated.

Tony frowned. "As I said, it's a small town.

If I told the driver I'd give you the package..."
He shrugged again, implying the rest. The driver
wasn't going to not deliver a package.

"Using a national shipping company to transport drugs made it easier for the FBI to track
them," Johnny said.

"Roger shipped them. How else...?" Tony
shook his head. "It was never supposed to get
out of hand."

Ellie took a step toward him, a headache forming behind her eyes. "But you lost track of a package because I never stole—"

Johnny gently touched her arm and gave her a
warm half smile.

Ellie felt her face flare red. She had so many
questions. Since her life had been thrown into
turmoil, she deserved the answers, but she had
to be patient and allow Tony to talk.

Tony lifted his eyes to her face. "The missing
package?"

Ellie nodded. "I never saw it."

Tony's Adam's apple worked in his throat. "I
stole it."

She caught her breath and Johnny gently
touched her hand.

"I thought I could make more money if I sold
the drugs instead of getting a flat fee for receiv-
ing the drugs. It was *only* one package." Looking

a little shell-shocked, Tony mopped his forehead with a shaky hand.

"Roger realized the package was missing before you had a chance to move all the drugs." Johnny's tone was even, commanding.

A sheen of sweat glistened on Tony's forehead as he bowed his head in silence.

"And you threw Ellie under the bus. Telling Roger that she had the package."

"Did Ashley know?" Ellie asked, annoyed at the squeaky quality of her voice.

Tony's eyes flared wide. "Oh, no. She didn't. I was afraid Roger was going to hurt one of you."

"You made sure Ashley was too busy to work in the shop."

"I wanted to keep her close, so I could protect her." Tony wrung his hands. "I tried to protect you, too."

Ellie felt all the blood rush out of her face.

"I wanted Roger to think that I was working hard to find the package." Tony shook his head in disgust. "Roger is an impatient man. When I didn't bring him the package, he started pressuring me. Threatening that he'd hurt my dad."

Tony dragged two hands through his hair, leaving it a mess. "I told him I'd look for the package. I couldn't just hand it over or he'd be on to me. How would I explain that the package was missing some drugs? I was backed into a corner. After he attacked you in this storage room, I knew I had to step it up. I hired that Kerry kid from the church to scare you. Throw a brick at the door. Shoot the front of the shop. I had to make it look like I was actively trying to get the drugs back. I thought it would hold Roger off. But when I didn't produce the package, Roger took things into his own hands. Breaking into your apartment… Attacking you in the yard…"

"But you were near the yard when I was attacked." Ellie's mouth grew dry at the memory.

"Yeah. I held Duke back so you'd go out looking for him." He shrugged, looking much younger than his years. "I didn't have a choice.

"I was in too deep. Once I created the lie, I figured if Roger found out, he'd kill me or my father." Tony shook his head in disbelief. "I couldn't find a way out."

"What did you plan to do? You couldn't have kept this up forever." Johnny's eyes grew cold. "Your plan was foolish."

Tony looked up. "You're telling me. I had sold some of the drugs and I knew there was a way Roger could have tracked them back to me if word got out." He fisted his hands. "I was trying to stall things until I could figure a way out."

"Roger took care of that for you," Johnny said with an air of disbelief.

"His patience ran out, even after I confessed."

Tony bowed his head; the defeat evident in the curve of his shoulders. "I was trapped." He glanced up, desperation in his eyes. "Roger's relentless. He kidnapped Ashley. I couldn't tell him I had lied, but I suspect he already knew. I was just doing everything I could to keep us from getting shot then and there."

"So you let him kidnap Ellie?" A muscle ticked in Johnny's jaw.

Tony rubbed his wrists, raw from the duct tape ripped from his flesh. "Did it look like I *let* Roger do anything?" His forehead creased. "You saw me. He had me tied up in there."

"You could have told the truth a long time ago," Ellie said, all the fight draining out of her. "You could have put an end to this a long time ago."

"I'm putting an end to it now. The package is in the freezer in the bakery. Get it out of there before anyone else is hurt." Tony hung his head. "I can't believe Roger almost killed me tonight."

"If I hadn't gotten away from Roger…" Ellie rested her hand on Johnny's forearm, needing an anchor. "If Johnny hadn't arrived in time, all of us would have been killed tonight."

"Thanks for carting me all over tonight," Ellie said as she and Johnny entered the old Victorian on Treehaven Road. She kicked off her shoes and lifted her eyes to the antique chandelier hanging in the entryway. The wonder in Ellie's eyes when she took in this grand old place always got him thinking. Thoughts better left for another time.

"My pleasure." He smiled.

"I forgot a few things when I stayed here. It should only take me a minute to grab them." She ran the palm of her hand over the smooth oak banister. They both knew she could have retrieved the items another time, but it seemed they both were looking for a reason to extend the night.

Johnny was sorry she was no longer staying here. He liked having her close by so he could keep an eye on her. But with Roger and Tony's arrest, she was no longer in danger.

But that's not the only reason you want her around, is it?

Johnny had never allowed himself to get this close to someone and for the first time, he was starting to understand the benefits of relationships far outweighed the potential downsides. If he could survive his mother's drug overdose when he was twelve, he could survive anything.

"Let me see where my grandfather is." Johnny checked the downstairs family room where Buddy normally watched TV, but his worn recliner was empty. Duke was nowhere to be seen, either. "Maybe he's upstairs."

"Oh, I hope we don't disturb him if he's gone to bed early."

Ellie climbed the staircase and Johnny followed. The distinct clicking of Duke's steps on the hardwood floor called his attention down the hall toward his mother's old bedroom.

Johnny's stomach pitched, the way it always did when his thoughts turned to his mother. He gently touched Ellie's back, not quite sure how he felt about having Ellie go into his mother's room. The room that until recently had been closed up.

Obviously sensing his unease, Ellie looked at him with a gaze that warmed his heart. "Why don't you go say hello to your grandfather while I collect my things?" Ellie reached down and patted Duke's head. The animal nuzzled his head into her leg. "Hey there, Duke. I'm going to miss you."

"You going somewhere?"

Johnny turned around to find his grandfather standing in the doorway of his mother's former bedroom. Johnny plastered on a smile even though his insides were rioting.

"What's going on?"

His grandfather waved his hand. "Glad you're here. I could use your help carrying these boxes downstairs."

"You're working late," Johnny said.

"I got a second wind, I suppose."

Ellie started to move toward the guest room to grab the things she had forgotten when his grandfather called out, "I could use your opinion, Ellie. If you don't mind?"

Ellie met Johnny's gaze and asked a silent, "Is it okay with you?"

Johnny took her hand and together they entered his mother's room. In the time capsule of a bedroom, his grandfather had the closet opened wide, a few boxes on the floor and clothes spread over the bed.

His mother's clothes.

"You've been busy," Johnny said, trying to keep his tone even.

His grandfather nodded.

"We made a few arrests tonight." Johnny squeezed Ellie's hand.

His grandfather smiled, a hint of pride glinting in his eyes. "I knew you would."

Johnny's mouth slacked and he laughed. "You already know."

"Living in a small town has its benefits."

"Seriously? How?"

"One of my friends called. He had just picked up a sub down the street from Ellie's gift shop." He tipped his head toward Ellie. "He saw the commotion and one of the officers filled him in. Glad to know you're okay. Both of you."

"Thank you." Ellie released Johnny's hand and

hugged her arms around her as if she were reliving tonight's events.

Buddy waved his hand. "I don't want to keep you. I'm sure Ellie wants to get home and put up her feet. She's been through a lot. But I need her opinion real quick."

"Sure." A crease lined the fair skin of Ellie's forehead.

"Do you think these clothes are appropriate to donate to the church? I know some people have hit hard times, but I don't want to offend anyone by giving them junk."

Ellie strolled over to the bed and fingered a jean jacket with beading around the front pockets. A memory slammed into Johnny: his mother's smiling face pushing him on the tire swing in the yard, the sun reflecting off the shiny beads on her jacket.

He shook his head, trying to dismiss it. He had always assumed that was a dream. A vision of a mother he'd wished he had. "Was there a tire swing hanging from one of the trees in the yard?" He hoped his voice sounded calm even as his pulse raced in his ears as he waited for the answer.

A slow smile spread across his grandfather's face. A light came into his eyes that Johnny hadn't seen in a long time. "Yes." He laughed. "You loved to swing. I had never heard a child giggle as much as you did when your mother pushed you on that swing."

The soft touch of Ellie's hand on Johnny's arm brought his attention to her face. She smiled, her eyes shiny with unshed tears. He placed his hand over hers and squeezed.

"Your grandmother had the swing taken down after your mother took you away. She couldn't bear to look at it." Buddy inhaled deeply and held out his hand, obviously eager to change the subject.

"So, Ellie, do you think any of this stuff would be good for a family in need at the church?"

Ellie smiled. "Absolutely. Kids today love this stuff. What's old is new again, right?" She touched a few more items. "Someone would be thrilled to receive these things. And if we can't find a deserving home, we can always sell the items at our spring bazaar. All proceeds go to a women's shelter."

Johnny's grandfather shook his head as if a decision had been made. "Great. Then perhaps, Johnny, you can help me carry the items to the garage for now."

"Sure." Johnny swallowed around a lump in his throat. Something shifted in his heart. Perhaps his grandfather's willingness to move on had pushed him in the same direction.

Ellie patted his arm and he looked down at her.

And Ellie certainly helped, too. "If it's okay, I'll run and grab my things."

"Sure."

Ellie turned and slipped out of the room. The golden retriever got to his feet and followed her out.

"I think Duke's sweet on Ellie," Buddy said, laughing and lifting a knowing eyebrow. "Don't let that one go."

"Ellie's got a pretty independent streak. I don't think she's one to settle down." He cleared his throat, staring at his mother's clothes from a lifetime ago. "She's been burned in the past..." Just when he realized he was spouting off every imaginable excuse as to why Ellie and he couldn't have a future, he found his grandfather studying him with a strange expression on his face.

"You about done?" His grandfather picked up the jean jacket, cast it aside and sat on the edge of the bed. "You can't keep living in the past. Your mother made her share of mistakes. I've made plenty of my own." His mouth twisted into a wry grin. "Don't *you* go and make the biggest mistake of your life."

"I don't—"

His grandfather lifted his hand, silencing him. "You've been chasing ghosts. Trying to rid the world of drug dealers, the kind of people who hurt your mom. You've done a great thing, but don't let that be the only thing you live for. You need to live your life."

A knot eased between Johnny's shoulder blades. "When did you get so smart?"

Buddy looked up, a sadness deep in his eyes. "Age and experience. I've had a lot of alone time to sit and think." He shook his head ruefully. "You don't want to end up all alone."

The clack of Duke's nails on the hardwood took his attention to the open door.

Ellie slowed as she approached the doorway, as if she suspected she was intruding on a private conversation. "Um, are you ready to go?" she asked Johnny.

"Of course," Johnny said, a little too forced, considering the heart-to-heart conversation he had just had with his grandfather.

"You have all your things now?" Buddy asked, gesturing with his chin to the items in her hand.

"Yes, I think so. Thank you so much for putting up with me." Ellie crossed the room and extended her hand to his grandfather.

Buddy stood and pulled her into an embrace.

"Nice having you. Don't be a stranger, okay?" His grandfather smiled. "Neither of you."

Ellie stepped back and Buddy approached his grandson. He patted his cheek. "Remember what I said."

Johnny nodded. When they reached the foyer,

Ellie looked up at him. "Are you all right? That had to be hard seeing all your mom's things."

Johnny blinked slowly and smiled. "Yeah, I'm fine. Really." And he meant it.

Ellie angled her head in confusion before a slow smile crept across her pink lips. She leaned forward, hiding her eyes behind a veil of hair. "I better get home. Greg's supposed to drop mom off. She stayed through the week at Grace's request."

"Is it really over for good this time?" Ellie unlocked the door to her childhood home.

"Seems that way." Johnny stood behind her. Something about him seemed lighter. Perhaps it was the arrests of Roger and Tony or maybe it was the conversation with his grandfather. It was almost as if both Johnny and his grandfather had come to some sort of reconciliation regarding the past.

She pushed open the door and the musty smell of a closed-up house greeted her. "My mother will be happy to come home. I think staying at Greg's was fun, for a while. But she enjoys her space."

Johnny followed her into the kitchen.

Ellie grabbed a couple mugs out of the cabinet. "They should be here shortly. I appreciate your staying to talk to them. My brother's going to have a hard time swallowing the news that his friend would be so stupid to get caught up in drugs again."

"It's not unheard of."

"True." She turned to face him. "Tea?"

"Why not?"

"I'm fine. I'm fine," Ellie's mother could be heard saying as she came through the back door. She dropped some grocery bags on the counter next to Ellie and sighed. "Ah, it's great to be home."

Greg followed her in with her suitcase. "Can I run this into your room, Mom?"

Their mother waved her hand. "It's got wheels. I can manage."

Greg braced his hands on the back of the chair in the kitchen. "Roger's been arrested?"

"Yes," Johnny said.

"Anyone else involved besides Tony?" Greg asked.

"He had gotten some kids involved with harassing Ellie, but other than that, I think we've put a dent in the drug trafficking business in Williamstown for a bit."

"I really thought Roger had changed." Greg slowly shook his head as if Roger's failings were somehow his own.

Ellie playfully punched her older brother's arm. He had always been the Golden Boy, even in her eyes. His confession had taken some of the shine off him, but she wanted more than anything to go back to the way things were. To make things right with the world. Perhaps that could never happen, not with all they'd been through, but they had to find a new normal.

Nancy Winters smiled at them both. "'For a righteous man may fall seven times and rise again.'" She extended the handle of her suitcase and rolled it across the worn linoleum floor. She pointed with her free hand at her son. "I'm proud of both of my children even when they fall." She slowed and patted her son's cheek. Ellie knew that Greg had confided in their mother over his past and she had obviously found a way to forgive him. Perhaps her age and faith had given her the ability to do so.

Nancy set the suitcase upright and wrapped her arms around Ellie. Ellie squeezed her back. "Feel good to be home, Mom?"

Her mom smiled. "It'll be nice to sleep in my own bed." Still hugging her daughter, her mother whispered in her ear. "I'm so very proud of you and how you've always handled yourself even under the most trying of times. I fear Dad and I may have let you get lost in the shuffle sometimes."

Ellie blinked away the tears. "No, Mom. I know you guys loved me. You had your own difficulties to handle, too."

Her mother cleared her throat. "Maybe you could use a little help around the shop."

"That would be nice." Ellie's voice cracked.

"Love you." Nancy gave her one more squeeze before letting her go. "I'm going to get settled in." She shivered with a contented smile on her face. "Excuse me." The wheels on her suitcase squeaked across the floor. She slowed in the doorway leading down the hall to her bedroom. "Lock up when you leave."

"Okay, Mom," Ellie said, feeling more settled than she had in a very long time. Ellie turned off the burner under the kettle. She was happy her mother had made peace with the situation and was ready to move on. Or at least have a good night's sleep.

"Well," Greg said, "I guess that's my cue to leave." He turned to Johnny. "I'm glad you got the bad guys. These kids don't realize how dangerous drugs are. They think they're invincible." He shrugged. "I guess that was my problem. I had thought I could do no wrong and the lines between right and wrong got blurred." His gaze shifted to Ellie. "I'm sorry I put you through all this. That I ruined your plans to go to college."

Ellie didn't say anything. She just leaned over and kissed her brother's cheek. "Night. Make sure you give Grace a kiss good-night for me."

"Will do." Greg turned on his heel then turned back around. "Will I see you around, Johnny?"

Ellie felt her cheeks heat as she found herself waiting for the answer.

"My assignment here with the FBI is done, but I do plan to extend my vacation to help my grandfather with some projects around the house, especially now that he seems open to the idea."

Greg looked as if he was going to say more, but didn't. He pulled the door closed behind him and the kitchen suddenly felt very close.

Ellie rolled up on the balls of her feet. "Well, Agent Rock, thanks for keeping me safe."

A lopsided grin curved his mouth. "The pleasure was all mine." He stepped closer and cupped her cheek, running the pad of his thumb across her soft skin, leaving a trail of awareness in its wake.

"What are your plans now?" he asked, his voice gravelly.

"I guess it's time I finally made a go of the shop. I have a few new ideas to turn things around." Once Ashley had a few days to recover, Ellie'd have to talk to her business partner. Maybe it was time to go to a bank for money and not rely on friends. She was determined to prove she could make it on her own. Be independent.

Her feelings must have been plain on her face

because Johnny asked, "What is it?" He stepped back, the smile slipping from his face.

"You're a really nice guy…"

He frowned. "Is this the brush-off?" He lifted an eyebrow in a semiamused gesture, as if he couldn't believe it.

She planted her hands on his solid forearms. "Don't consider it a brush-off. I'm just looking for time."

Johnny nodded slowly. "I understand."

"And there is the issue of our jobs. You in Buffalo and me here in Williamstown."

"You can always find an excuse." His eyes lingered on hers.

Suddenly self-conscious, she dropped her hands from his arms and stepped back. "I know. But knowing that I can do something on my own is important to me. I need time."

Johnny smiled and stepped closer, brushing a kiss across her lips. "I'll be back," he said in what she suspected was his best Arnold Schwarzenegger impersonation. She smiled.

I'm counting on it.

The minute he closed the door, Ellie hoped she hadn't just made the biggest mistake of her life.

EPILOGUE

Four months later...

Ellie lifted the canvas, placed it on the easel and stepped back. Six easels sat in two neat rows so that all of her clients for her first Get Out and Paint class could easily see the demonstration. In the front of her shop, she still carried a few gift items and greeting cards, but for the most part, she had transformed her run-of-the-mill gift shop into a fun, night-out destination for ladies, couples and even children's parties.

A rap at the door called her attention. The guests weren't supposed to arrive for fifteen more minutes. She had set out fruit and vegetable platters, refreshments and chocolate-chip cookies, sure to be a big hit with the teens from her church who were scheduled to paint tonight.

Ellie smoothed her hands down her apron and turned toward the door. Her heart stopped.

Johnny.

They had called each other a few times over the past few months to check in, but nothing more than that, and Ellie had begun to wonder if her quest for independence had been shortsighted.

Walking toward the door, Ellie did her best to keep her expression neutral. She had missed him. She turned the dead bolt in the door and opened it wide. A cold January wind whipped into the room.

Johnny stepped inside and stomped his snowy boots on the gray floor mat inside the door. "Looks like you're having a party." He stuck out his lower lip, feigning disappointment. "And I wasn't invited."

"Didn't much think you'd like to travel from Buffalo on a snowy night to paint a sunset." She placed her hand on her neck to cool her skin, which felt as if it was on fire despite the cold blast of winter air. Tilting her head, she couldn't contain her smile. The expression "a sight for sore eyes" sprang to mind.

"A painting party?" His eyes brightened with curiosity. "So, you went and did it. You followed through with your plans to transform the shop."

"Yes, yes, I did. People book painting parties," she said, an air of pride filling her lungs. "I still have a small gift shop, but my focus is on these parties."

Johnny walked slowly to the back of the shop

and plucked a grape from the platter before popping it into his mouth. "Interesting."

"Yeah, you'd be surprised how many people are willing to come out of their houses just to get away and do something creative."

"Nice…" he said, nodding, a smile on his handsome face.

"I'm really enjoying painting more, too."

"Bonus," Johnny said, his brown eyes studying her, unnerving her.

"And…" She found herself rambling. "I've enrolled in some weekend classes on Saturday at the nearby college campus. They have a fantastic art education program. I've hired Kaylee to cover the shop. My mom offered to help, too."

"Isn't that what you hoped to do before—?"

"My plans got derailed." Ellie nodded. "Just goes to show you, it's never too late to figure out who you are."

Johnny reached out and ran a long strand of her auburn hair through his fingers. "You're not exactly ancient."

"No, I suppose not, but I've taken my share of knocks."

"And come through it remarkably well."

"Thanks to my faith."

"Thanks to you, I've come to realize how important faith is, too. I've come to peace with a lot of things in my past. And with my mother. What did I once hear you say, 'You have to let go and let God'?"

Ellie smiled. "One of my favorites."

"How's Ashley?"

"Fine, we're still friendly but I don't see her as often as I used to. We're no longer in business together. I drew up a business plan and was able to secure a bank loan. Can you believe it?"

"Of course I believe it." The confidence in his statement filled her with pride. He really did believe in her.

A long silence stretched between them before Johnny finally said, "I'm sorry it's been so long since I've stopped by."

"I told you I needed my independence." An emotion she couldn't quite name made her voice shaky. "You respected that."

"I did." His voice softened. "But it wasn't easy."

Ellie tugged on the collar of her shirt at a loss for words.

A coy smile split his face. "Is it okay that I've stopped by tonight?"

She nodded. She *had* proved to herself that she could create a successful business. She smiled politely, trying to act nonchalant. "So, what brings you to Williamstown?"

Johnny opened his mouth to speak when the bells on the front door jangled.

Kaylee and one of her friends bustled through the door and came up short when they noticed Johnny and Ellie engaged in a serious discussion.

"Are we early?" Kaylee asked, her cheeks flushed pink from the January cold. She was holding a box from the bakery next door.

"No, no…you're not early. And you didn't need to bring food." The smell of freshly baked cupcakes reached her nose and her stomach growled. "But we'll definitely enjoy those." Ellie smiled. "We'll start when everyone gets here."

The two girls giggled as they moved toward the refreshment table.

"Mr. Vino's still able to run the bakery?"

"Yes. I've helped him coordinate with the church to employ young people. It's hard to find a job in a small town and if the youth are busy working at the bakery, they might stay out of trouble." She smiled at how far she and Mr. Vino had come since their stormy introduction. "One of the kids is great at computers. The bakery even has online ordering and shipping. Business has really picked up, or so he tells me."

"Nice. Maybe the business will still be around when Tony gets out of prison in a few years. Maybe he'll have a second chance to continue his family's business."

"Maybe. But for now, the teenagers Mr. Vino

employs really seem to enjoy working there. I've decided I can't worry about much more than today."

"Sounds like a good life motto." Johnny smiled, then gently took Ellie's elbow and moved her all the way toward the front of the store. His tone grew serious. "I've missed you."

Ellie tugged on the collar of her turtleneck again, thinking it couldn't possibly get any hotter in her small store.

A playful twinkle danced in his eyes when her response was slow in coming. "This is where you're supposed to say something like 'I've missed you, too.'"

Ellie coughed and covered her mouth. "Of course. Yes. I have. I've missed you."

"This wasn't the reception I imagined." He laughed.

She shook her head, confused. "I just thought with me committed to Williamstown and you in Buffalo and traveling for your job…"

"I've been permanently assigned to Buffalo. I won't be traveling as much."

"Oh."

"And since it's not that far, I figured maybe…"

The girls giggling by the back table caught her attention, but when Ellie looked at them, they were staring at their phones, apparently engrossed with something on the screen.

"I'd love to take you on a date, Ellie. I mean, if you have time with your new business and school."

Biting her lip, she looked up, meeting his warm gaze. Wasn't it time she made time? Trusted a man?

"I'd love to go out on a date, Agent Rock."

He cupped her cheek and laced his fingers through her hair. The bells on the door clacked again. She started to turn toward them when Johnny smiled. She couldn't take her eyes off him. He bent and brushed a soft kiss across her lips. He pulled back and asked, "What time are you done tonight?"

"Seven."

"I'll be back at seven, then."

"Okay." Warmth coiled around her heart.

Johnny stopped with his hand on the door. He jerked his chin toward the bright orange wall at the back of the store. The day she had painted it Citrus Blast seemed a lifetime ago. She couldn't help but think of Collin and Kerry who were currently in a youth program to get them on the right track.

"Ellie?"

The concern in his voice shook her out of her reverie.

"Have you done any painting lately?"

"You mean walls?"

"Yeah?"

"Not since I set up the shop."

Johnny gave her a quick nod. "Well, I might need some help."

Ellie stared at him, angling her head in confusion.

"I'm thinking the commute from Williamstown to Buffalo isn't too far."

Her heart thumped against her ribs.

"And my grandfather wouldn't mind the company."

"You're moving into the old Victorian on Treehaven Road?"

A slow smile crept across his handsome features.

"And I was thinking maybe you'd like to help me pick out the colors when I paint. Update the place a little."

Ellie felt light-headed. "Why?" whispered out.

Johnny pressed a kiss to her lips. "I'm hoping maybe someday down the road you'll be living there, too." His lips moved against hers as he spoke.

She pulled her head back, breaking the kiss. "Is this a proposal?" Her forehead crinkled, but she couldn't help but smile.

Johnny cupped her chin and did that thing with his thumb on her cheek again. "Not yet, Miss Ellie. Not yet."

She felt her face flare hot. "I didn't m-mean..." She found herself stammering.

"But one day soon...one day soon."

Johnny winked and pulled open the door. The bells jangled. A rush of air entered the space, cooling her fiery cheeks.

Ellie turned and found Kaylee and her friends beaming at her in a way only teenager girls could. The rest of the girls must have slipped in while she was distracted.

Excitement bubbled up inside Ellie and she strode toward the easels set up in the back of the shop. She handed each girl a brush and some paints. "Let's get started. Who's ready to paint?"

Kaylee giggled and straightened her shoulders. "You are so lucky, Miss Ellie."

Ellie smiled. "I like to think I worked hard to get to where I am today." She touched the young girl's hand. "Remember that. Work hard and be patient." Ellie ran her hand across the edge of the blank canvas. A blank slate. The future was hers to create.

Kaylee was too polite to roll her eyes, but Ellie sensed that's what the young girl wanted to do.

Ellie laughed. "If you remember nothing else..." She searched the young girl's eyes. "Have faith. Trust in God that things will work out."

Ellie glanced at the front door. Johnny had just made a promise of a future together. Butterflies flitted in her stomach. Her gaze drifted to the clock on the wall.

Seven o'clock couldn't come soon enough.

* * * * *

Dear Reader,

I hope you enjoyed *High-Risk Homecoming*. This is my fifth release from Harlequin Love Inspired Suspense and if you've had a chance to read my other books, you may have noticed I've set all of them in fictional small towns near Buffalo, New York.

I am proud to have been born and raised in Buffalo, the home of chicken wings, the Buffalo Bills and the friendliest people. Even after going a thousand miles south for college, I found my way back, albeit to a suburb of my hometown. Even my brother, who spent twenty-plus years in New York City after graduating from NYU, has made his way back "home" recently to raise his young family.

It is this sense of home and belonging that draws me to write about Western New York. *High-Risk Homecoming* is set in Williamstown, my fictional version of the Village of Williamsville, one of my favorite places just outside Buffalo. Williamsville has unique shops and coffee houses lining its Main Street. It is on *my* version of Main Street that I gave my heroine a gift shop. Here, she finds herself the target of a ruthless villain and, thankfully, under the protection of a handsome FBI agent. Not a bad tradeoff!

If you ever have a chance to visit Western New York, be sure to check out our unique architecture, including Frank Lloyd Wright's Martin House, our beautiful waterfront and the perennial favorite, Niagara Falls.

Thank you for taking the time to read my book. I truly appreciate it. I hope you'll look for more of my titles. I love hearing from my readers. I can be reached at Alison@AlisonStone.com.

Live, Love, Laugh,

Alison Stone

LARGER-PRINT BOOKS!

GET 2 FREE LARGER-PRINT NOVELS
PLUS 2 FREE MYSTERY GIFTS

Love Inspired®

Larger-print novels are now available...

REQUEST YOUR FREE BOOKS!
2 FREE WHOLESOME ROMANCE NOVELS IN LARGER PRINT
PLUS 2 FREE MYSTERY GIFTS

∗∗∗∗∗∗∗∗∗∗∗∗∗∗∗∗∗∗∗∗∗∗∗∗∗∗∗∗∗

HEARTWARMING™

∗∗∗∗∗∗∗∗∗∗∗∗∗∗∗∗∗∗∗∗∗∗∗∗∗∗∗∗∗

Wholesome, tender romances

YES! Please send me 2 FREE Harlequin® Heartwarming Larger-Print novels and my 2 FREE mystery gifts (gifts worth about $10). After receiving them, if I don't wish to receive any more books, I can return the shipping statement marked "cancel." If I don't cancel, I will receive 4 brand-new larger-print novels every month and be billed just $5.24 per book in the U.S. or $5.99 per book in Canada. That's a savings of at least 19% off the cover price. It's quite a bargain! Shipping and handling is just 50¢ per book in the U.S. and 75¢ per book in Canada.* I understand that accepting the 2 free books and gifts places me under no obligation to buy anything. I can always return a shipment and cancel at any time. Even if I never buy another book, the two free books and gifts are mine to keep forever.

161/361 IDN GHX2

Name _____ (PLEASE PRINT)

Address _____ Apt. #

City _____ State/Prov. _____ Zip/Postal Code

Signature (if under 18, a parent or guardian must sign)

Mail to the **Reader Service**:
IN U.S.A.: P.O. Box 1867, Buffalo, NY 14240-1867
IN CANADA: P.O. Box 609, Fort Erie, Ontario L2A 5X3

* Terms and prices subject to change without notice. Prices do not include applicable taxes. Sales tax applicable in N.Y. Canadian residents will be charged applicable taxes. Offer not valid in Quebec. This offer is limited to one order per household. Not valid for current subscribers to Harlequin Heartwarming larger-print books. All orders subject to credit approval. Credit or debit balances in a customer's account(s) may be offset by any other outstanding balance owed by or to the customer. Please allow 4 to 6 weeks for delivery. Offer available while quantities last.

Your Privacy—The Reader Service is committed to protecting your privacy. Our Privacy Policy is available online at www.ReaderService.com or upon request from the Reader Service.

We make a portion of our mailing list available to reputable third parties that offer products we believe may interest you. If you prefer that we not exchange your name with third parties, or if you wish to clarify or modify your communication preferences, please visit us at www.ReaderService.com/consumerschoice or write to us at Reader Service Preference Service, P.O. Box 9062, Buffalo, NY 14240-9062. Include your complete name and address.

HWI5